SAILING BACK TO ELLIS ISLAND
The Enjella® Adventure Series

Praise for
Sailing Back to Ellis Island

"Abigail and Bennett return in a smart, nimble mix of history and fiction for older elementary- and middle-grade readers. The siblings—gifted by fairies with the ability to fly, shrink in size, become invisible, and speak various languages—journey to Ellis Island...

Drawing upon her own family history, interviews, and historical documents, Collen provides a vivid picture of the events experienced by so many people that came to America, relating their hopes and fears, the crowds they encountered, the health inspections they endured, and the challenges they faced regarding language and cultural differences...

A well-researched, lively volume that leavens the Ellis Island experience with humor, fairy-tale magic, and an appealing plot."

—Kirkus Review

"This edition will surely spark the interest of 8th grade social studies students and inspire further reading..."

–P. Zeidan, high school teacher

"Curious minds who enjoy learning about history and the diverse cultures that make up America will relish *Sailing Back to Ellis Island*. Kids and their parents will find themselves connecting and caring for the immigrant families arriving in the United States for the first time and negotiating their entry into the country. The engrossing immigrant tale sails by with thoughtful, meticulously researched details about Ellis Island and healthy doses of fairy fun. As a narrative lead, Enjella—a multicultural renegade tooth fairy turned heroine—is the perfect escort into this moving story of America's immigrant past, and the timing for this novella could not be more relevant today."

—Marcy Clark, Women's Mafia editor

"The book puts a fanciful spin on the often arduous and incredibly tedious process that immigrants endured upon entering into the new land: America pre-World War I. . . This time traveling tome is perfect for the young reader in your life who is just beginning to learn about American history. Plus, for us brown girls; it can serve as a great introduction to some of the more troubling and more personal part of history."

—Karla Borders Pope; founder BrownGirlGumbo

"Accomplished illustrator Trumble's (Twinkle, Twinkle, 2014, etc.) witty, full-page drawings and visual accents are a fine match for the text."

—Kirkus Review

SAILING BACK TO ELLIS ISLAND
The Enjella® Adventure Series

By Jane F. Collen

Illustrated by David Trumble

Streamline Brand Associates, Inc.

Printed in the United States of America

Print Edition ISBN 9780985573263

Visit www.Enjella.com for more information

To: Our Immigrant Ancestors who left us their magical stories

And to my wonderful, supportive, loving family of willing readers and editors.

Contents

CHAPTER ONE

A Mysterious Note

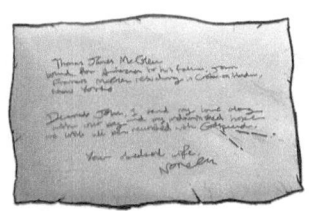

ZAAAAAP! A scrap of paper appeared out of thin air and fastened itself to the pajamas of the sleeping boy.

Two Fairies materialized in the darkened bedroom, twinkling, glowing and giggling; floating over two sleeping children.

Rustle, crackle, sigh. The two children dreamed on.

The eleven-year-old boy, Bennett turned over in his sleep, felt something prick him and woke up.

"OUCH!" he sat up. "What is this weird pin doing on my shirt?"

The tiny Fairies burst out laughing, doing somersaults in the air.

"Is this a clue to where we are going tonight?" Bennett greeted the Elbow Fairies with his question. He crossed his legs underneath him and stared at the piece of paper pinned to his pajama shirt.

Enjella and Alicia, the Elbow Fairies, came to visit Bennett and his sister Abigail almost every night. The Fairies had befriended the children a long time ago when the children still had baby teeth and the Fairies were still Tooth Fairies. In fact, the reason Enjella and Alicia quit the Tooth Fairies and started the Elbow Fairies in the first place was because they wanted to get to know and help these children; they no longer wanted to just gather teeth.

This week the Fairies were giving history lessons, taking Bennett and Abigail on magical learning adventures.

Enjella, the president of the Elbow Fairies, touched down on the girl's pillow. Abigail bolted upright, fully clothed, and shouted, "Where ARE we going tonight?"

Enjella shot off the bed leaving a trail of nervous sparkles. "You startled me!" she cried.

"We are just too excited!" said Bennett, bouncing up on his knees. "Last night's adventure was amazing. I can't wait to see what we are doing tonight." He took another bounce and flew up into the air.

The magic sparkle streaming from Alicia's wand caught Bennett in mid-flight and moved him back over the bed, just in time for him to avoid taking a header.

"Whoa-ha! Slow those horses DOWN cowboy." Pop! A cowboy hat appeared on everyone's head as Alicia spoke.

"Slow down? No way!" said Abigail. "We have tons of energy thanks to all the sleep we got when we returned from our adventure last night. Your magical movement of time is the BEST."

"Enchanted Elbows! You are awfully conscientious!" said Alicia. Pop! Many hands appeared all over Abigail's head and patted her.

Unperturbed by the distraction, Enjella returned to Bennett's first question and told him, "Yes! Our destination tonight has something to do with the note pinned to Bennett's shirt."

Abigail peered over her brother's shoulder and scrutinized the paper he had just unpinned. Bennett studied the note for clues too. "What language is this?" he asked.

Abigail examined the Fairies' apparel. Enjella was dressed in a long skirt, topped by a wide scarf that she wore like a sash, a peasant blouse and a shawl. Alicia was wearing a Dirndl dress – the traditional dress for women of Germany a century ago.

Under Abigail's gaze, Alicia took a walk along an imaginary fashion runway, rose in a graceful pirouetting turn, and flew back in front of her.

"It's pretty obvious where we are going, right Kiddo?"

Abigail shook her head no.

Enjella laughed, "It's as plain as paper!"

Bennett looked up from his continued inspection of the note. "Nothing is plain! I still can't figure out what this says. I mean, I recognize some words so it must be in English, but the writing is so strange I can't understand it."

Alicia's head sported her Sherlock Holmes hat. A magnifying glass appeared in her hand. She inspected the paper.

Looking scholarly in horned rimmed glasses, wearing an old fashioned button down shirt with a pocket protector attached, Enjella explained, "It's elementary my dear Watson! You are a boy immigrating to the United States from Ireland in 1908. Your father went to America ahead of your family to work to earn enough money to pay for all of you to join him. He has just sent the funds to cover all the transportation costs. Your mother is expecting another child any day now and is not able to make the journey. So she pinned a note to your jacket for your father, kissed you goodbye and sent you along with one of your aunts to set sail for America."

Bennett's mouth dropped open in shock.

Abigail nudged him and whispered, "You'd better close that yapper before…"

ZAAAAP! Alicia tapped a fly into existence, which made a beeline for Bennett's open mouth.

WHAAP! Enjella's wand became a fly swatter and smacked the fly back to the magic kingdom of New Sparkleshire, the home of the Elbow Fairies. She twinkled at Alicia, but steam came from the top of her head. "Always with the shenanigans!" she complained.

Unperturbed, Alicia danced a little jig floating in the air over the children's heads.

"I'd have to go all by myself? But I am only a kid!" Bennett said.

"Life was very different then," Enjella advised. "People had to make many hard choices, and children often had a great deal of responsibility, all by themselves."

"But that still does not tell us where we are going," said Abigail, scratching her head.

"We are headed to the United States headquarters for processing immigrants from 1880 to 1945…"

"A drum roll please!" Pop! A drum and a fully uniformed drummer, with a top hat and tasseled drumsticks, appeared out of nowhere, floated over their heads and gave them a drum roll.

Enjella rolled her eyes, but then drew in her breath to give a dramatic pause. She announced, "Ellis Island."

Wham! A cymbal crashed and the drummer disappeared.

Alicia and Enjella each tapped a child on the elbow and they all disappeared from the children's bedroom in a flurry of sparkles.

"But I have to change my outfit!" Abigail lamented from thin air.

CHAPTER TWO

Arriving at Ellis Island

"Cool! This time we flew across time and space all at the same time!" said Bennett. He straightened his wind swept hair and looked with awe at the dark, foreboding towers in front of him. The imposing structure was the main building on Ellis Island. The children landed on a gravel path next to the water's edge. The Fairies hovered next to them.

Abigail looked blank and a bit dazed from the travel. "What?" she asked. "Where are we?"

"Don't you mean WHEN are we?" teased Alicia.

Bennett tried to explain, "We flew back in time and to New York at the same time."

"Shouldn't you say 'simultaneously'?" Enjella asked. "I think it is less confusing than using 'time' twice in the same sentence."

A map appeared in Alicia's hand. "You say this is New York? I say Ellis Island is in New Jersey!"

The Four Time Travelers looked down at the map.

"The original three-acre island was in New York. But it was expanded two times using dirt and debris from ship's ballasts and the excavation of the New York City subway system. When the island was expanded in 1892 to twenty-eight acres, most of the new part was in New Jersey," informed Enjella.

"So the actual land came from New York, but they dumped it in the Hudson river on the New Jersey side of the border between the states. You should have heard the uproar when the two states fought in court to determine who owned this important island and the Statue of Liberty," chortled Alicia, slapping her knee. Pop! She was dressed in flowing judges' robes and holding a torch.

"Who does own it?" asked Abigail.

"Like any good neighbors, they agreed to share!" said Enjella. The group studied the state line drawn right through the island on the map.

TOOOT TOOOOOOOT!

The children jumped in alarm. The Fairies flew straight up into the air, startled into releasing a stream of sparkles. The group whirled around to see a ferryboat chugged directly at them, aiming for the dock.

"That was right in my ear!" shouted Bennett.

Abigail clamped her hands over her ears as the boat blew its whistle again. Deck hands roused themselves from their resting positions around the dock. Official looking men appeared from a nearby small wooden structure. The main doors of the imposing building in front of them opened and another official stepped out, looking at his pocket watch.

The History Explorers could see passengers leaning out of every opening in the two-story barge. Some people were cheering, shouting and pointing. Others stared silently, searching the dock with anxious eyes, travel-weary and unsure of what was to come next. In a quick movement that jarred the ground, the barge hit against the wooden planks and pilings that served as a pier at the end of the gravel path. The Time Travelers jumped again.

With the help of the deckhands, the boat was docked and the gangplank was hustled out and secured.

Almost instantly, people of all shapes and sizes appeared on the gangplank. They carried heavy bundles, bags and suitcases and poured off the boat. The passengers wore the colorful clothing of many different cultures from many different countries. Uniformed men stationed at the end of the gangplank looked at the numbers pinned to the people's clothing and pointed them in the direction of the large doors.

"How did you know we went back in time?" Enjella asked the children.

"Any doubt I may have had was erased by one look at those clothes," answered Abigail. "Ladies were certainly well-covered then. I never imagined they wore so many layers of petticoats, skirts, coats and coverings! And even though some ladies look very fancy and others are practically wearing rags, all the ladies have hats."

Abigail looked again and then corrected herself, "Or some form of head covering." She pointed to a lady with a shawl on her head. The shawl had so many fringes that the tassels fell across her forehead like bangs.

"What year is it anyway?" asked Abigail.

"I'm guessing it is over a hundred years ago, because there are no utility lines and that ferryboat looks so old fashioned," announced Bennett.

Alicia made a quick flight down the dock, past the buildings, and zipped back again. "I think that was a lucky guess. Ferryboats today don't look much different than these barges. It could be last year."

"True," said Bennett. "But you said we were going to 1908."

"Good listening Bennett!" approved Enjella.

"And I thought you were half asleep," said Alicia. Pop! An old-fashioned nightcap appeared on her head. A snore of ZZZZZZZZZZs fluttered over her.

"Where are the cars?" asked Bennett. "I would love to see a real live Model T."

"The good old Model T Ford!" exclaimed Enjella. Pop! She and Alicia wore strange white caps, big goggles, huge workman's gloves and scarves.

"What is that get-up for?" asked Abigail.

"Standard driving equipment for the operators of the first motorized vehicles," said Alicia, adjusting her goggles.

"That's right!" Bennett snapped his fingers. "There were no windshields. The cars only went about 15 miles per hour, but it got pretty breezy."

"Well, sorry," said Alicia, the goggles and caps disappearing from their heads, "you won't see any here on this island. In 1908, while there were some cars, they were very expensive. The most common mode of transportation was still by ship."

One of the ferryboat sailors began to whistle, "*Take Me Out to the Ball Game.*"

A second sailor sang back, "*Take me out with the crowd.*"

"The Ball Game song was around in 1908?" asked Bennett.

"It was one of the most popular songs of the year," confirmed Alicia, baseball cap on her head and a package of CrackerJack appearing in her hand.

"They had CrackerJack then?" said Abigail.

"Of course! It's in the song!" said Bennett. "Buy me some peanuts and CrackerJack," he sang, along with an official who was singing while he worked. The uniformed man was pointing his finger at the crowd and then pointing in the direction of the main Registry Building to move everyone along.

"Ahem!" whispered Enjella, pointing down to the crowds of people.

The Time Travelers turned their attention back to the landing.

A family with two little girls, a big steamer trunk, many small bags and some things bundled up in beautiful cloths, brushed by the Fairy group. They looked bewildered by their surroundings. In spite of each carrying what looked like a heavy bag, the two little girls held each other's hands, and stared with big eyes at the crowds of people rushing around them. Officials stepped closer to the family, pointing and shouting instructions, hurrying the passengers toward the big doors.

A scrawny boy with a moth-eaten cap gazed in awe at the elaborate architecture of the enormous building in front of him. The woman he was with tugged his arm to move him along. The children did not notice him, but Enjella pointed him out: he had the note! That same mysterious note that had appeared pinned on Bennett's pajamas.

"There he is!" Alicia laughed and shone a flashlight on him as she pointed with a long stick in her hand.

"Gee!" said Bennett. "The note belonged to a real kid, who really left his mother behind, and immigrated here, accompanied only by his aunt!"

"Thomas McGlew," affirmed Enjella.

Bennett and Abigail's delight at seeing the owner of the note was interrupted by a shout from below.

"Vat my American name?" called a man. The children saw a short, skinny man with a scraggly beard, lugging a huge bundle on his back shouting in a happy voice to an official.

"Whatever you say it is!" laughed the official.

"I vant America Name," he declared.

"Smith? Vanderbilt?" joked the official as he pointed to the big doors and tried to move him along.

"No much American," the man insisted.

"Then take Roosevelt!" the first official said. "If it is good enough for our President, it is a great American name!" He gave the man a poke to keep him moving toward the entrance.

"Ja, ja!" the man smiled and stumbled forward saying, "Rose-velt, rose-velt."

Bennett and Abigail looked at each other. Bennett shrugged his shoulders and raised his hands, mouthing, "What was that about?"

A woman with seven children, colorfully dressed and all carrying bundles, caught their attention next. "There are lots of kids on that barge," Bennett whispered. "And these kids are walking in height order!"

"How many different languages are being spoken at the same time here?" Abigail asked. "Where is everyone headed? What do they have to do now?"

"Are some kids really traveling all by themselves, without their parents, or even an aunt?" Bennett said, with concern in his voice.

"Questions, questions!" crowed Alicia, doing cartwheels in the air. Pop! Question marks hung from her hair and clothes, bouncing at dizzying angles and glistening in the sun. "I love inquisitive questions!

"YES!" she finally answered after she ended one more tumble with a big WINGS UP sign. "There are lots of languages and lots of children! And some of them get into a little bit of a pickle…"

"Precisely!" said Enjella, wearing an inspector uniform; a miniature replica of the one the officials were wearing. "As we have established, the year is 1908. Several large steamer ships have just recently arrived in the port of New York. No one is allowed to set foot on the ground until they have been cleared for landing by the United States border authorities. This ferryboat carries passengers from the ship's third class or 'steerage' section. They are brought here to Ellis Island to be examined by the United States Immigration Officers to see if they conform to the Immigration Law standards."

"Wait! Why only the third class passengers? What happens to first class and second class passengers?" asked Bennett.

"AH HA! He is paying close attention!" clapped Alicia. Pop! A graduation cap appeared on Bennett's head. "Those passengers are interviewed and inspected on board the ship, in their cabins, once the ship docks in Manhattan."

"What kind of inspection?" asked Abigail.

"Everyone had to show they were healthy…" Enjella began.

"And if they are unhealthy," Alicia interrupted, flying in front of Enjella to get Bennett and Abigail's attention, "they would have to submit to further tests on Ellis Island, or go to its infirmary."

Enjella glared at her. "Let's not get ahead of ourselves, shall we? As I was saying, healthy first and second class passengers are cleared onboard the ship to land. After the legal confirmation of their paperwork, they get to leave the ship right from the dock in Manhattan."

"Goodness!" said Alicia, "We would not bother to travel all this distance, and all this TIME if we were only going to lecture you about something you can find on the Ellis Island website. We came here to show you instead."

Enjella did an Irish Jig to fly in front of Alicia… "A-HEM! As I was saying: Our mission today is not just to experience what it was like to immigrate to the United States in the early 1900s, but also to help a few of the immigrant children."

"First," said Alicia, once again flying in front of Enjella, "we will follow this ferry load of people as they pass through the whole immigration process. We will accompany them through all the different tests in the various parts of the building."

"Tests? I didn't study for any tests!" Bennett joked to Abigail. She made a silly face in reply.

Enjella disappeared for an instant before reappearing in front of Alicia.

"Now," Enjella smiled. She tapped both Bennett and Abigail on the back and they instantly shrank to half their size and sprouted Fairy wings. "You are invisible, and must fly close to me and my cohort Alicia at all times. Zip along now. We have much to see and much to do."

"But what are we…" the words trailed behind Bennett as Alicia pulled him forward by the elbow. They flew over the thick crowd of new immigrants laden with unwieldy bundles streaming toward the massive front door entrance to the grand building.

"Zip it!" commanded Alicia in a whisper, out of the side of her mouth. "I said we were invisible, not inaudible." An image of a robotic fairy appeared above her head and said, "Please hold. Your questions will be answered in the order in which they were asked…"

Bennett looked puzzled, but did not dare to say anything. As the History Explorers flew down the wide path he concentrated on observing all the people who were advancing slowly in line below him.

Abigail nudged him as they flew along. She could not stop herself from whispering to Bennett, "This looks like a gigantic costume party."

CHAPTER THREE

New Country, New Life, New Name

"It sure is crowded and noisy in here," Abigail shouted. They were in the baggage room, just to the left inside the big doors.

"This is the first stop…" Enjella began, but she realized the children could not hear her.

"Where did everybody come from?" Abigail shouted. The huge main building, which had looked so silent from the outside, actually resounded with noise and teemed with people. Workers shouted to each other and gave instructions to the immigrants. Officials pointed and shouted. People talked in multiple languages. Babies cried. Mothers scolded. The line of newly arrived passengers slowly approached baggage workers who ticketed their bags and gave them receipts. Behind the counter the many trunks, suitcases, odd sized packages and bundles were all stacked in rows or heaped in piles on the floor.

"What?" Pop! A big horn appeared in Alicia's hand and she put it to her ear.

"What the heck is that?" Bennett scratched his head, as they hovered over the bustling crowd.

"What the heck is what?" Alicia put the horn back to her ear.

Bennett shouted into the horn, "What is THIS?"

Alicia flew back as if blasted away and a startled stream of sparkles emanated from her head. "Wow! This crazy contraption really works! You almost shouted my ear off!"

"It looks like part of an old fashioned music box, the part that was a sound amplifier," said Bennett.

"Exactly right! I am trying to blend!" shouted Alicia.

"Aren't we invisible?" laughed Abigail.

ZAAAP! Enjella's wand whipped out and back, almost too quickly to be seen. The horn disappeared from Alicia's hand. The objection forming on her lips disappeared too, when she saw the look Enjella gave her.

Enjella laughed and shot some sparkles into the air. "Ok, I know this antique stuff is fun, but we have lots to observe and do here. Let's not get side tracked."

Pop! A train car, complete with tracks, appeared on Alicia's head. Suddenly a second set of tracks appeared. As the children watched in amazement, the train pulled over to the second set of tracks and stopped. Another train sped by on the original tracks, blowing their hair straight back with the wind it generated before disappearing into oblivion. The first train then slowly began to creep forward, moved onto the track just occupied by the speeding train, and chugged off into thin air.

Bennett and Abigail just stared, amazed.

"So that's what the expression 'side tracked' means!" Bennett laughed.

Their conversation stopped as their Fairies whisked them toward a grand stairway. They hovered over the heads of the people laboriously beginning to climb the stairs, some still carrying their baggage.

Why didn't they leave their bags at the bag check? Abigail wondered.

As if Enjella could read her mind she said, "As you can see, some of the new arrivals did not trust the bag check system. I guess if I left my home forever and only brought a few possessions, I would probably be afraid to surrender them to the baggage room too. It is such a big, strange, chaotic place with no easily intelligible organization system. It does not inspire confidence in the security of the bags."

"Vat my American name?" someone shouted.

The Time Travelers turned and flew back toward a man stopped in front of one of the officials in the baggage room.

"Hey look! It's that same guy!" exclaimed Bennett. "Why does he want to change his name?"

"Many people had their names changed because of clerical errors made by the shipping company when they prepared the written ship manifest or passenger list," explained Enjella. "Other immigrants had problems being understood, either because they could not understand or speak English, or because the officials did not understand their accents and got their names garbled. Most people had never seen their names written in English before. In some instances, the inspectors could not read the names written on the line. They only had a few minutes' total time to assess the immigrants' qualifications to be allowed to enter, so they had no time to linger over the immigrants' names."

Bennett and Abigail looked puzzled so Alicia explained, "There was a two-minute legal inspection to screen out any immigrants that did not seem fit to enter the United States." Bennett and Abigail nodded their heads.

"Wow! What a short amount of time for such an important decision!" said Bennett.

"It is easy to see why some names got jumbled. But for most people, their names were changed because they wanted to assimilate into their new country. They wanted to Americanize their names," said Alicia. Pop! Three pinwheel firecrackers fizzed on her head. "Maybe they figured: new country, new life, new name."

"Nein, nein." The group looked below them to see the man with the scraggly beard shaking his head. "Herr President?"

The official scratched his head, "Well our American President is Mr. Theodore Roosevelt, but what does that have to do with you?"

The man smiled, "Rose-velt, Rose-velt. Ikh shoyn fargesin."

Alicia and Enjella twinkled and giggled.

"What does that mean?" Abigail asked.

"You will see," the Fairies both said, giggling and shooting sparkles out of their wands.

ZAAP! The Fairies pulled the children by the elbows and flew them quickly up the grand staircase. Enjella cleared her throat. Pop! Her hair pulled itself up into a neat bun and teacher-ly half glasses appeared on her nose.

"Now, children, you must use your powers of observation..." Enjella began.

"That is not very specific!" Alicia put her hands on her hips indignantly, her face red with annoyance and her hair red and sticking out every which way. "Shouldn't we be telling them what to look for?"

Enjella winked mischievously, pulling down her glasses and showing her laughing eyes. "Nope! It is more fun for me if they have to guess!"

The Fairies floated the group back down the staircase.

"Hey! Why in the world are we going down this enormous staircase when everyone else going up?" Bennett interrupted.

"We zoomed you right up to the top of the stairs so you can see what they see," Enjella said unhelpfully.

"What who sees?" demanded Abigail.

"The health inspectors," said Alicia. Pop! A burlap bag appeared over her head, and out walked a cat.

"She let the cat out of the bag!" said Enjella, who hovered with her back to Alicia.

"We can see THAT!" said Bennett and moved his hands to indicate Enjella should twirl around and see.

Abigail giggled. "Well we haven't learned that much about immigration yet, but we are sure learning a lot about English expressions."

Enjella stamped her foot in the air. "I am trying to teach you! I have a very advanced teaching style: I allow you to observe and then I interpret what you see. But SOME Fairy..."

Alicia giggled. "Interpret! That is the perfect word to foreshadow what will happen later." The children stared at each other in confusion. Enjella had a mysterious smile.

"We are watching the doctors of Ellis Island watch the immigrants." the information burst out of Alicia. "As the new arrivals walk up the grand stairway to the main processing room, the health inspector doctors are already at work conducting an initial screening."

"How do they do that?" asked Bennett.

"They check to see how healthy the people look; how do they carry themselves? Do their eyes look ok? Do they have runny noses? Are they coughing or wheezing? How well do they walk as they climb the stairs?"

Bennett and Abigail looked skeptical. "They could tell if the immigrants were sick from just those signs?"

"At a glance, the doctors can see if the people are invalids, if they have rickets, if they have problems with their spines, problems with their lungs, or something wrong with their legs. The doctors had a few seconds to check for evidence of over 60 symptoms. The system was actually quite efficient." Pop! Alicia's hair separated itself into six neat rows. Simultaneously six clumps of hair started weaving itself into braids. "The immigrants have to climb the stairs to the second floor anyway. So rather than making them line up a separate time to walk in front of the inspectors, they view them in action now."

Pop! A ticking stop watch appeared in Enjella's hand. "This allowed the second part of the exam to last about 20 seconds," she said. She pushed the knob at the top of the watch with her thumb and the clock's hand stopped on the twenty second mark.

"But what if they are tired, or their feet hurt? Doesn't that look the same as being sick or unable to walk?" asked Bennett, his nose wrinkled with worry.

"Or what if they just have new shoes?" asked Abigail. "I got blisters once from new sneakers."

Alicia somersaulted in the air. "You are getting the picture! It is very hard to assess this many people quickly and efficiently, yet fairly, to decide if they are qualified to enter our country.

"It was an inexact science to be sure. There was a big margin of error and a lot of room for misunderstanding," Enjella confirmed. "And that is before you add in the translation problem."

At the top of the stairs, doctors marked some of the people with chalk.

"What's the chalk for?" Bennett whispered, as they hovered over everyone's heads.

"People are marked when the doctors notice something that needs further checking. Those people will be pulled aside, detained in those areas over there and later brought to an examination room for a more thorough screening."

"Ugh," said Bennett. "It looks like they put those poor people in cages."

"In 1908 they processed from 2,000 to 10,000 people every day! There was no time for niceties. Everything was done as quickly as possible," said Alicia.

"This is very intimidating," Abigail declared. She scanned the crowd. "I don't see any 'W' for 'can't walk'."

"'L' for 'Lame'?" Bennett, scratching his head, guessed.

"Excellent deduction Sherlock!" said Alicia. She tapped his head with her wand and her Sherlock Holmes hat appeared on Bennett's head. Pop! Three more hats materialized in the air. Alicia juggled them, in and out of her hands, and on and off her own head. "'Lame' was the medical term used then to indicate any problem with walking, or in general with the legs or back."

Into the upstairs Grand Hall the people streamed, lining up in front of another set of doctors. The health inspectors stopped each person in turn, checked each closely and asked a few questions. Within two minutes the inspectors either marked the person's coat or jacket with chalk and sent them to a waiting area caged with wire fences, or dismissed the person to continue down the line to wait for the legal inspection.

The History Explorers stopped to listen to an inspector question an immigrant.

"If I give you two dogs today, and then tomorrow another officer gives you two more, how many dogs would you have?" asked the inspector as he scrutinized a man.

The man standing before him hesitated. The inspector glanced briefly at his document for the man's name, and asked him again. "Ah, Pat, if I gave you two dogs today, and someone else gave you two dogs tomorrow, how many dogs would you have?"

Pat gave a big grin and replied, "Seven."

The inspector frowned, marked him with an X, pointed him in the direction of a detainment room and moved to the next person.

"What does 'X' mean?" asked Bennett.

"'X' means he is marked for potential mental problems, and will have to be further examined," explained Enjella.

"But maybe he did not understand!" said Bennett.

"Do you think he spoke English?" Abigail fretted.

"He sounded like he was from Ireland," said Bennett. "Maybe he did not understand the inspector's accent?"

"Maybe not," said Enjella. "It was the inspectors' duty to make sure the new immigrants would be able to take care of themselves in America. They had to be healthy enough to be able to work and provide a living for themselves. Anyone who was not mentally capable would be considered likely to become dependent on the state, or a nuisance to society. These people were detained and then sent back home."

"So Pat might be sent home?" Abigail asked, concerned for the poor man.

Alicia twinkled and laughed. "He could have been, but luckily…" she paused.

Bennett and Abigail looked at each other in confusion.

The Fairies tapped them on their elbows and in an instant, they were in a room that looked like a courtroom.

"We are just b-bopping around in time," announced Alicia. Pop! Clocks appeared, dangling from her ears, perched on her head, and hanging from her wand. Hands of analog clocks spun around furiously and numbers flashed with urgency on digital clocks. "It is a day later, and we are going to show you what happens to Pat."

The children recognized Pat sitting silently in a row with other immigrants. All of them wore grim faces.

An inspector called Pat to the front of the room. He stood, nervously fidgeting in front of a panel of three officials who all stared at him with purposeful and businesslike expressions on their faces.

"Pat, if you are given four chickens and then a fox eats three, how many chickens will you have?"

Pat answered, "One chicken, sir, that's the sad state o'it."

"Oh good!" said Abigail. "But why. . .?"

"Shhh. Listen," said Enjella. Pop! Big lips with a finger in front of them appeared over her head.

The inspector asked Pat several other math questions and he got them all right. Then he was asked to read a paragraph from a book. Pat stumbled a bit, but he read it through. And then they asked him to write his name, and home address.

"Well, Pat," said the inspector, "you seem to be reasoning just fine now." The other men on the board nodded in agreement, although still without smiling. "Further, you proved you could write and read adequately enough. So answer me just one more question. If I give you two dogs, and when you leave here we give you two more, how many dogs will you have?"

"Seven," Pat said without hesitation.

Everyone looked at each other. The children got worried again.

"Now Pat, are you sure of your figuring?" asked the inspector with a frown, as the two other men on the panel scratched a big line across the papers in front of them, and shook their heads 'no'.

"Sure and Begora, I am certain," declared Pat, giving the official a big goofy grin.

The inspector scratched his head. "I just can't understand your arithmetic."

"Why it's simple," said Pat, "Yer giv'n me two dogs today," and he held up two fingers, "and you'll be giv'n me two dogs tomarra," he held up two more fingers on that same hand, "and them dogs, coupled with me own dogs I already own," and he held up three fingers on his other hand, "make seven."

All of the inspectors and the children burst out laughing.

"Thank goodness Pat was given a chance to explain," said Abigail as she breathed a sigh of relief. The Fairies touched the children's elbows and whisked them all back to the Grand Hall.

"Ikh shoyn fargesin"

The Time Travelers zipped around the perimeter of the Grand Hall, looking at the groups of people huddled in the corners and on benches. Their
wings all drooped as they passed the sad sight of people detained in the
areas fenced in like cages. The middle of the room contained long lines
of immigrants, walking through what looked like pens, carrying all sorts
of bags and bundles. At the far end of the Registry Room, at the end of
each long line, stood a tall imposing desk with an even more imposing
inspector looming behind it. The immigrants shuffled with nervousness
as they waited for their turn to appear at the desk.

The children giggled constantly as they eavesdropped on bits of con-
versations here and there. They zoomed from line to line, listening. One
little boy stood in his family group shouting, "Mama! Mama!" He pressed
closer to his mother, tugging on her skirts. "Samuel, hush now, what
troubles thee?" the woman said, bending down toward him. His mouth
made a surprised round "o" shape and his voice squeaked as he marveled,
"Mama! So many legs! America has so many legs."

Bennett screeched to a halt in front of little Samuel. "Wait, why can
we suddenly understand everybody?" he asked.

"Magic!" Pop! Paperbacked dictionaries appeared on the top of Alicia's head. "We have concocted a special Fairy translation spell. Enjella knew we were going to need a very hard-working, persevering, diligent, tenacious, persistent, determined, meticulous and painstakingly accurate spell. We have to be able to decipher all these old languages and decode the different dialects. So, Enjella combined all the existing modern language translation spells, added an old decryption and an old interpretation spell, put in an extra measure of SPARKLE and perfected an incantation just for this occasion.

"And," Alicia paused dramatically. Pop! Banners unfurled out of thin air. "TAT-TA-TA-TAAAA!" Trumpets flourished. "I named it… The Un-babble-ator!"

The children looked totally unimpressed with the name.

"Don't you get it?" A tower appeared on her head, encircled with ramps. "The word 'babble' comes from the biblical story about the Tower of Babel: Men were trying to build a tower tall enough to get to heaven to be on the same level as God. The Bible says that Yahweh changed every man's language so people could no longer cooperate and join forces to build the tower."

"This is an education," said Bennett. "But in linguistics! Not in immigration history."

"Everything is related! Languages always change and evolve. New words come into languages almost every day. People create new words to describe current events, designate new customs and label new inventions," said Alicia with a triumphant cartwheel

Enjella concluded, "That is why we had to make an extra special translation spell. Some of the languages spoken just a hundred years ago have changed so much that people now-a-days might not understand them."

The children looked a trifle bewildered. "Gee," said Abigail. "I thought magic was just… magic."

"Who would have thought you'd have to cogitate and calculate to do magic?" agreed Bennett. 'This is all so complicated,"

"Yes," agreed Abigail, "this whole trip is a little overwhelming."

"An ancient proverb says, "The longest journey in the world begins with a single step," reassured Enjella.

"An apt metaphor for watching emigrants," laughed Alicia.

Bennett and Abigail flew to the desk of an inspector at the end of one of the long lines of immigrants. The Fairies hovered nearby.

Group after group arrived at the desk. Time after time, the inspector read the number pinned to each immigrant's coat. He ran his finger along the ship's manifest until he found that number on a line. Stumbling, he attempted to pronounce the immigrant's name. The immigrants each presented their medical and legal papers to the official. The inspector examined the documents, comparing them to the information written on that line of the manifest from the ship. As he reviewed the documents, the official spot-checked their accuracy by asking each immigrant a few key questions.

When he was satisfied with the answers and the paperwork, the inspector wrote out a landing card and stamped the papers, waiving the people through. "Go down the right side to the ferry," he said, again and again.

After each group, the inspector rubbed his eyes under his glasses and sighed.

"NEXT!" he called.

The newly admitted immigrants always hesitated, as if unable to believe they had been accepted into the United States. But as the inspector immediately busied himself with straightening his papers, inking his pen and reading the manifest while waiting for the next group, the immigrants picked up their bundles and walked toward the stairs.

"Next!" the inspector called again, absentmindedly leafing through the many pages of the manifest as he looked down the line at the seemingly endless stream of people.

"The people just keep coming!" said Bennett.

"Yes," said Abigail, "They are lined up all the way back to the stairs."

A woman wearing a pretty scarlet and purple dress, scarlet headscarf, a white wool coat and a multicolored shawl stepped forward.

"Isn't she hot wearing all those clothes?" whispered Abigail.

"Probably!" answered Enjella, "but if she wears her coats, she won't have to carry them – and look at how much she is carrying already." The woman had a huge bundle tied in a big woven-wool blanket. "Probably everything she owns is in that package."

"Papers!" said the officer briskly, staring at the manifest of the ship VADERLAND from Antwerp, Belgium, open before him.

"Name!" he said without looking up.

"Mein Nommen ist Dirdack," whispered the woman. "Sarah."

"You are seventeen years old? Where are you from?" the inspector asked, turning the page of the manifest and running his finger through the information listed next to her name.

"Dirdack," Sarah whispered again.

"You own the town?" the inspector looked up and laughed shortly, but with a kind expression on his face.

"Are you traveling alone?"

Sarah did not reply, but then pointed to herself and said "me."

"Translator!" shouted the inspector, looking around.

A nicely dressed lady appeared at his side. "The translators are all busy. As you know, I speak five languages," she said.

The American woman turned to address the petite immigrant trying to peer over the top of the inspector's desk. "I am from the National Council for Jewish Women, and I can help you," she said in Polish. The woman's eyes grew larger, and she bobbed her head up and down, but did not say anything.

"How does she know this lady is Jewish?" whispered Abigail.

"The aide societies of different faiths organized and sent relief workers daily to meet most ships," explained Alicia. "They would find out what ships were docked, and send women over to help."

"I am Cecilia Greenstone," the woman said to Sarah in Yiddish. "I founded our aid society. Do you understand me?"

"Of course!" said Sarah proudly, "My father was a Rabbi. I have an excellent education, better than some of the boys in my town. I am fluent in Yiddish and Hebrew, and I speak a little Polish."

"This will be easy then! Whom do you come to meet?"

"No one!" said Sarah.

Cecilia Greenstone frowned. "Perhaps not so easy."

She faced the inspector, "The Jewish Women's Aide Society will give this woman a home and help her find gainful employment. She will stay

with us in New York City."

"Nein, nein. Massachusetts." Sarah pointed to herself.

Cecilia Greenstone looked at the small immigrant in surprise. "What do you mean?"

Sarah rapidly said, in Hebrew, "I was given instructions to travel to Holyoke, Massachusetts. There I meet my betrothed at the house of his family. There he works, I work. "

Cecilia turned toward the inspector and translated. "This woman is traveling alone. She is engaged to be married to an honest man living and working in Holyoke, Massachusetts. She has instructions to meet her betrothed there, in the home of his family."

"We release no single woman to wander the streets without a man to look after her or without any source of income." The inspector shook his head. "You know this well: We cannot admit anyone likely to become a ward of the state."

"I am perfectly well acquainted with procedure, sir. We at National Council for Jewish Women, joining with our sisters at Hebrew Immigration, are prepared to vouch for this woman and ensure that she arrives safely at the home of her betrothed and is duly wed." Mrs. Greenstone drew herself up to her full height and squared her shoulders, as if to do battle.

"Now, Mrs. Greenstone, you know you cannot be sure this will occur, much less than personally guarantee it on the basis of one conversation of less than five minutes duration." The inspector frowned over his glasses at her.

"I can tell from this woman's grammar and elocution that she is very well educated. The National Council will provide this woman with food for her journey, and make sure she has carfare. We will also insure that if for some reason she encounters problems reaching her destination, or marrying her betrothed, she will be able to contact us and we will pay to have her returned to us to find alternative useful employment and shelter."

Mrs. Greenstone set her jaw firmly. The History Explorers could see that she was determined to win Sarah her entrance into the country.

"Ticket," said Sarah in Yiddish, "I was sent a ticket for the railroad."

Mrs. Greenstone smiled at Sarah and took her hand. "That makes things much easier. I should have asked you in the first place." She turned to the inspector and switched back to English. "The family is expecting her, they sent her a prepaid ticket."

"Very well," said the inspector. "If you could assist me with corroborating the answers for our twenty-nine questions?" he barely waited for Mrs. Greenstone's nod of her head. "At the conclusion of our examination, if I am satisfied that… " he peered down at the manifest and lifted up his glasses to see better, "Miss Dirdack's answers match her previous statements which have been recorded and notarized on the manifest, and if you commit to overseeing the future of this woman, I will release her to you so you can ensure she is reunited with her family."

"Has anyone threatened you or forced you to promise to marry this man you are betrothed to?" the inspector asked as he adjusted his glasses and began again. Mrs. Greenstone translated, and Sarah answered, very calmly, and with a fierce concentration, choosing her words carefully.

"Do you have an address where we can contact him and advise him of your arrival?"

Sarah's papers were stamped and she was sent down the right side of the Stairs of Separation to the Railroad Ticketing Office and Waiting Room.

The team floated away. The children began to pepper the Fairies with questions.

"Why does Sarah have to prove she is marrying someone in America? We saw men coming in, and all they had to prove was they had some money and they were going to look for a job. It's not fair that a woman has to prove she will have someone to take care of her!" Abigail put her hands on her hips, just warming up to her subject.

A red light appeared over Alicia's head and a full traffic light flashed yellow on top of Enjella's.

"Stop right there!" commanded Alicia, police gloves on her hands and whistle in her mouth. "Women don't have many independent rights in the United States in1908. They don't win the right to vote until 1921."

"It is certainly not fair!" Bennett took up the cause. "I saw a group of men use the same twenty dollars over and over again to prove they had enough money to pay the "head tax" and enter the country! Someone on the other side of the fence passed the dollar bills down the line; each man could hold it, if they paid the owner of the money twenty-five cents, to show to the inspector when it was their turn. And they were approved!"

"Entrepreneurship!" chortled Alicia, and slapped her knee.

"More than entrepreneurship, kindness and public service are valued by Americans," declared Enjella. "Mrs. Greenstone, along with many other sons and daughters of immigrants, started organizations to help the people who left all the comforts of their home, their way of life and every familiar thing they ever knew, to start a new life in the United States."

"Luckily your Great Grandmother has a lot of chutzpah. She got herself, with only a little help from the Jewish Immigration society, all the way from her home town in current day Lithuania to Holyoke, Massachusetts, even though she did not speak a word of English," twinkled Alicia with a happy smile on her face.

"Our GREAT Grandmother?" the children gasped and looked at each other.

"We never got to meet her!" said Abigail. "Do you think she looks like us at all?"

"I THOUGHT she looked a little familiar!" said Bennett.

"Can we see her again?" asked Abigail.

With a touch of her wand, Enjella whisked them all to the bottom of the Stairs of Separation. They had a great view of Sarah Dirdack walking calmly, with her head held high, down the right side of the stairs, chatting in Hebrew with Mrs. Greenstone.

The Time Travelers watched them check the posted ferry schedule. Mrs. Greenstone walked Sarah to the door. Sarah drew a deep breath and straightened her shoulders. The last view her great grandchildren had of Sarah was of her stepping out the door to the ferry, standing as tall as her five-foot frame would allow. She was on her way to the train station in New Jersey, ready to start her new life in America.

The children and their Fairies cheered. Everyone made the WINGS UP sign, fingers fluttering happily. In mid-hooray they found themselves back at the top of the stairs in the Registry Room.

"What is called the president of the United States?" the Fairy team looked down from their celebration to see that same man asking yet again about the name of the President.

"Mr. Roosevelt?" answered the official, "We call Mr. President: Mr. Roosevelt."

"Ja Roseveld!" the man smiled and continued down the line.

"Does he have a problem with his memory?" asked Abigail.

"Will they mark him with an 'X'?" worried Bennett.

"Yes and no!" laughed Alicia. Enjella chimed in laughing and said, "Look below and listen!"

The inspector called, "Next!"

The inspector checked the man's papers; everything, including his medical inspection, was in order. He asked to see his money.

"Fifty-four dollars!" said the man proudly.

"All right Mister…" the inspector paused as he scrutinized the page trying to read what was written on the manifest. "Uh, what is your name?"

"Mein Nommen!" the man tapped his head as if he were trying to remember something. "Mein Nommen!! Ach!…shoyn fargesin!" the man muttered.

"All right then," the Inspector wrote out a piece of paper. "Mr. Sean Fergusson, welcome to the United States of America. You may go down the right side of the stairs to schedule your transportation to the main land."

The man looked puzzled, then pleased. "Sean Fergusson!" he stated, picked up his bag and hurried away.

Enjella and Alicia gave each other the WINGS UP sign.

The children looked at each other with astonishment written on their faces and asked, "But he said 'I already forgot,' how did they get 'Sean Ferguson'?"

The Fairies turned somersaults with merriment and laughter. "Don't forget, with the magic spell, you hear the English translation." Pop! A chalk board appeared and the words 'I forget = shoyn fargesin' appeared in sparkling letters. "He said 'shoyn fargesin' which the inspector heard as 'Sean Fergusson'. What devilish merriment!"

"But the inspector could see that the man was not from Ireland!"

Abigail protested.

"Yes," agreed Bennett. "He was in line with his fellow travelers from Russia and Belarus. Don't the inspectors know where the people come from?"

"Of course," answered Alicia. "The ships wait in port until they are told it is their turn to send immigrants over for processing. The immigrants are sent over in ferries, along with their ship's manifests."

"Ok," said Bennett. "So then why did they change his name? Plus! He was speaking Yiddish! The inspector should have known!"

"It was not the customs official's business to tell people they could not change their names. It was a different time, when it was easier to remain anonymous and keep off the grid. There was no time, nor any way to verify the statements made by the immigrants." POP! A ticking stop watch appeared in Enjella's hand again. "Remember, the officials simply compared the information collected by the shipping company, recorded on the manifest, with the answers the immigrants gave to the questions they asked them at their desks," said Enjella.

Alicia pointed to the long lines of immigrants and agreed. "Most of these people don't have any verifying documents. And look how many are still waiting to be processed."

Copies of the manifest appeared suddenly in each child's hand. "Look at the handwriting!" Alicia said. The children stared at the foreign-looking scrawl of words. They struggled to decipher anything written on the sheet.

"Arggg," said Bennett. "As if the full words were not hard enough to read, these abbreviations are impossible to decipher."

"Don't forget," warned Alicia, "time is still ticking away, and the lines are getting longer as you try to read this document."

The History Explorers looked at the lines and lines of people, all anxiously waiting to learn their fate. The stop watch kept ticking.

POOF! Suddenly the stop watch exploded and vanished. The startled group looked down the stairs. And laughed!

There was the newly admitted and newly named Sean Ferguson shaking hands with the railroad ticket sellers. Clearly over the din of noise in the Grand Hall, they could hear him say, "Ja, ikh bin Sean Fergusson."

CHAPTER FIVE

Children Are To Be Seen
And Not Heard

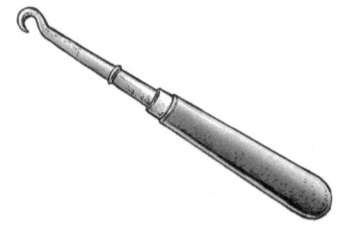

WAAAAH! Waaah! WAAAAAAAAAH!

The laughter of the Time Travelers over the new name of the man from Belarus was interrupted by the cry of a baby right below them. They had floated back towards the medical inspection lines at the top of the entry stairs. The health inspector plied the dreaded buttonhook to examine the crying baby's eyes for trachoma. The inspector pronounced the baby free of the disease, dipped the buttonhook into a jar of clear liquid, reached out and laid it on the eyelid of the baby's sister. With his other hand, the inspector pulled the eyelid of the older girl up and over the buttonhook with one quick motion, leaned in to look closely, and then released the eyelid. "Ok young lady, you are free to proceed." The older girl, wincing from the sting of the alcohol used to clean the buttonhook, blinked back tears and silently and bravely followed her mother and sister to the next part of the line.

"That is barbaric!" said Abigail. "Why do they have to do that? Do they pull up everyone's eyelids?"

"Ouch!" said Bennett.

"This was one of the more unpleasant but necessary parts of the health exam. The inspectors are checking for trachoma, a bacterial eye infection. Any person with red, puffy or bloodshot eyes had to submit to the dreadful examine."

"I never heard of that disease!" said Bennett.

"That is because a young immigrant from Japan grew up to be a scientist, and discovered a cure for it," said Alicia. Pop! A steaming beaker appeared in her hand and a scientific laboratory formed around her.

"But what was it?" asked Abigail, big-eyed with worry.

"It is a painful eye disease that causes inflammation and scarring on the eyelids, turning the eye inwards. It was highly contagious. If left untreated, the disease resulted in blindness or even death."

"It doesn't seem fair to keep someone out just because they are sick," said Abigail.

"The job of the inspectors was to make sure all new immigrants could take care of themselves, be productive citizens and not become a liability to the state. They needed to be healthy enough to be able to get a job. It was very difficult to get a job if you were handicapped in those days, since most jobs involved at least some physical labor."

"I'm glad we live now, and not then," Abigail shivered.

The History Explorers watched groups from another ship make their way along the long line of immigrants waiting to be processed through the short medical exam and then the legal inspection. A family of three people caught their eye; a dark haired man, his beautiful brunette wife and their little blond-haired daughter.

The man began to hum, "O Sole Mio" while they waited in the line and the little girl sang the words.

"Gee," said Bennett. "Who knew that song was so old?"

"Isn't that little girl pretty?" said Abigail, admiring the girl's long, golden, braided hair.

"Mama, wait," the little girl whispered to the woman next to her. The woman kept walking forward, her eyes fixed on the inspector's desk.

The little girl tugged her mother's skirt with one hand and her mother's arm with the other. Thanks to the magic translation spell, the children heard the whole dialogue in English: "Mama wait for me. Why are you going without me? Don't leave me behind!"

The woman leaned down and whispered, "When we get to the inspector's desk you are not to say a word. Papa will answer all of the important questions and you are just to remember your place. Children are to be seen and not heard. Bad mannered children are not welcome in America. I am counting on you to behave like the proper young lady you are."

"Si, Mamma. I will be a good girl. Can I just hold your hand?"

"Perhaps no. We must listen to the inspector and do as we are told." The woman straightened and picked up her bundles.

"Next!"

The trio stepped to the desk.

"Your name?"

"Scopatore."

The girl opened her mouth and repeated 'Scopatore'.

The inspector glared at her. So did her Mamma.

"Where are you from?"

Papa said, "Turbone."

The little girl said, "Tuscany."

The inspector glared again. "Which is it? Or are you from different places?

"Hush Francesca," the mother whispered, and she dropped her daughter's hand and glared at her again. Francesca made a face.

Laughing suddenly, the little girl grinned a devilish grin. Looking up at the grownups, she seemed determined to be part of the conversation. Once again when the inspector asked her father a question, Francesca gave a different answer using the little English she learned on the ship.

"How old are you?"

The father answered, "39." Francesca said, "30."

"Hush!" her mother said more sternly, and a little louder.

Francesca crossed her arms and looked down with a pout.

"Who is this little girl?" asked the inspector.

Francesca pressed her lips tightly together. The Time Travelers could almost hear her thinking, "If I am told to be quiet, then I won't say anything, but I am not going to be happy about it." She stayed quiet and round eyed.

"Gratzie! Non, Non, but my daughter Senor," said Mr. Scopatore, with halting English.

"She does not look like you!" announced the inspector, scrutinizing her carefully. "Furthermore, she does not resemble your wife, either. Not even faintly."

"I assume this is your wife?" the inspector asked. Francesca stayed silently pouting and her parents both nodded their heads yes.

"Did you get married so that this man would take you to the United States?" The inspector turned his attention to the woman.

"No, No, Prego!" the mother looked upset.

"Do you argue over many things? How well do you get along? Were you forced to marry this man? "

The adults struggled to answer these questions, exchanging bewildered glances with each other.

"Why is he asking these questions?" Abigail whispered.

"These are standard questions. The goal was to make sure their marriage was not arranged simply to provide the woman entrance to the United States," Alicia looked serious, her hair resuming its blue color, with a proper straight part, and well-combed look. Enjella had a clipboard and was checking off the questions.

"Is this your daughter?" The inspector turned back to the man.

"Tuto Bene! But of course Senor." The man looked surprised.

"Certamente! Securemente!" said the woman, which the children heard as 'of course, certainly.'

The inspector asked the little girl, "What is your name little girl?"

"Her parents can tell him that!" whispered Abigail. "He is going to scare her."

"The inspector has to ask the little girl her name," explained Enjella. "That's how they made sure the children were not deaf. And she had better answer him, or he will think she is dumb."

Alicia flew in between Bennett and Abigail. "Dumb as in 'can't speak'," she whispered in both of their ears.

"I got that!" said Bennett.

Alicia flounced away, "Huh, you think you are so smart. Did you also know, any child over two, even if their mother was carrying him or her, had to walk alone in front of the inspector, to prove he or she was not lame?"

Bennett and Abigail looked at each other and shrugged. "How would we have known that?" Abigail asked.

"I thought not," said Alicia. "So I will keep providing you with information, whether you show appreciation or not!"

Enjella crossed her arms and stared at the Francesca, as if willing her to speak and to behave. The little girl kept pouting.

The inspector said. "She does not answer. Can she hear? Can she speak? She does not look like you. No, I see no family resemblance to either of you. Did someone ask you to take this girl to America for him or her? I do not believe she belongs to you. She is not standing with you." The inspector looked around for a supervisor.

Francesca, still pouting, had turned her back to her parents and was now standing a bit apart from them.

"Pronto, pronto," Francesca's father was getting upset. "She just spoke before, when you asked the questions. Everything is in order. This is our precious little girl. She is properly listed on the manifest as our daughter."

"Do you have any papers to prove she is yours?" the inspector continued his line of questioning.

"Did they forget to bring her passport?" Bennett asked the Fairies.

"They don't have one!" said Alicia.

"How can that be?" asked Abigail.

"Passports were not required until 1952," said Enjella.

"What about her birth certificate? Why doesn't the man just show the inspector their documents?" Bennett asked.

"They don't have any," whispered Alicia, her eyes fixed on the drama unfolding before them. Pop! She was sitting in mid-air on a collapsible travel chair, eating popcorn as if she were at a sporting event.

Bennett and Abigail did not believe her.

Enjella whispered a further explanation. "Passports were not generally used. King Henry V of England created a document in the 1400s to try to ensure safe passage of his envoys to foreign lands. Many countries tried to help their citizens prove who they were, with official papers that identified them, but passports were only used sporadically. During wartimes, many countries requested documentation, but passports generally were not mandatory until after the Second World War. In most countries, before then, official passports did not even exist."

"Furthermore," Alicia said from her sports chair, between bites of popcorn, "most people did not have birth certificates. Most babies were born at home. There was no system for documenting most births. Adoptions were not done formally either – if something happened to parents, concerned friends and relatives would decide what to do with the children. They would either take them into their own homes – without any formal procedures or papers — or send them to orphanages."

"What are these people going to do?" Abigail whispered.

"Hang on," said Alicia. Pop! Old-fashioned subway straps appeared out of thin air. Abigail and Bennett each grabbed one, without thinking. "I think we are going to find out right now!"

"I 'ave no papers, but those I already give you," the man took off his hat and wiped the sweat from his brow. "Here is my number." He pulled the card pinned to his jacket off. "We are three persons!" He said in heavily accented English. "Together we travel. This is my daughter. I raised my bambino from the day she was born."

The woman started crying, "Me bambino."

"Alright now," said the inspector. "Mr. and Mrs...." He paused to look for their names again on the manifest, "Pascquale Scopatore, please approach my desk." The two parents stepped in closer. Francesca, still turned the other way with her arms crossed, did not even notice her parents move. The Time Travelers flew in closer too, because the inspector dropped his voice.

"I have an idea. You both must simply walk away from the desk. Proceed to those stairs. Do not look back or say anything to that little girl. If she is not your daughter, she will not react. She will probably remain where she is. If so, I will deliver her to my supervisor for deportation."

The woman gasped, but the parents did as they were told and moved away from the desk. Francesca, still pouting, did not notice!

The four adventurers looked at each other. "She will figure it out, right?" asked Bennett, his face puckered with worry.

Enjella and Alicia just shook their heads and shrugged with their raised arms.

"Oh no!" whispered Bennett, "when Alicia does not have a costume change, we know: that girl Francesca really is in trouble!"

CHAPTER SIX

Tongue Twisting Time

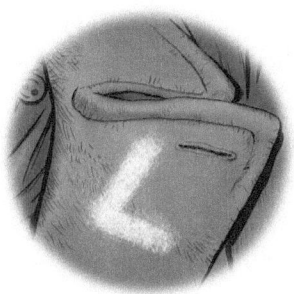

"We can't let this happen!" Abigail shouted, flapping her wings furiously toward Francesca.

Abigail flew right to the little girl's ear and whispered, "Run to your parents! Call them! Or you may never see them again!"

Startled, the girl looked up and saw her parents moving rapidly away, without looking back. She ran after them shouting, "Mama, Papa, why do you leave me? Mama, Papa, please wait! I was just playing."

The inspector smiled to himself, picked up his pen and motioned for the next group to step forward to the desk. "Number twenty-one," he read aloud from the tag pinned to the man approaching him, and scanned through his manifest pages.

The Fairy group breathed a sigh of relief. Pop! A big fluffy mattress appeared over Alicia's head. A transparent ghost of Alicia appeared above the mattress, put its hands behind its head and plopped down. A big whooooosh of air came out of the mattress and out of the ghost. Abigail and Bennett burst out laughing.

"My spirit feels like doing that too!" said Abigail. "I was so worried that Francesca would be separated from her parents and left alone in a strange world!"

Bennett said, "No. Worse! She would have been sent back!"

Enjella frowned. Pop! A traffic light, flashing a yellow warning light, appeared over her head.

"Aren't you happy that we helped prevent a total disaster?' Bennett asked.

"There are worse disasters ahead," said Enjella, shaking her head. "This one only required minor magic. We are going to need a major miracle-magic to help us with the big problems we came here to avert. There is potential for a mix up that would place both of your lives in jeopardy!"

As if on cue, a loud wail rose up from a child in the mass of people below. A baby's cry joined the wail.

"Hold on just one second," said Bennett, after seeing the baby comforted by its mother. "What do you mean, 'our lives are in jeopardy'?"

"Perhaps nothing!" said Alicia.

"One of the disasters we need to avert is something that could happen to your Great Grandmother."

"But we already saw her. We saw her buy her ticket for Holyoke, Massachusetts. I know that is where she lived; that is where my father was born."

"Don't forget," said Enjella. "You have FOUR sets of Great-Grandparents."

"Abigail and I have to make sure they ALL gain entrance to America?" asked Bennett with a worried look on his face.

Enjella did not directly answer his question. "So many dramas occurred in this hall. A significant part of many life histories were written here. So many nerves were stretched to the breaking point. The arduous journey was taxing enough on the immigrants; but on arrival there was the uncertainty of whether they would be turned away. Then, even if they were accepted, the immigrants still had to find a home, get a job, get established – start a new life. There was a lot of anxiety in this hall."

"Many children here could use your helping hand," said Alicia. Pop! A huge hand appeared over her head, scooped her up and rocked her. "Besides," she said lying back in the swinging hand as if it were a hammock, "most of the people here are somebody's grandparents."

"I want to help everyone!" said Abigail.

"That's the spirit," said Enjella. "You will definitely be helping SOME-ONE'S ancestors."

"But first," laughed Alicia, "some comic relief. Do you remember the note pinned to your shirt Bennett?"

"It was the start of our adventure," said Abigail.

Enjella pointed. "Right down there is that young lad again. The one who had the note pinned to his coat; the one who really did have to leave behind his mother and his home."

The children looked down. They saw the boy and a woman walk away from the inspector's desk and get pointed in the direction of the corridor to the right of the Stairs of Separation.

"Oh no!" said Bennett, "why are THEY being detained?"

"Don't worry," laughed Enjella. "They have been approved to land. They will go to the telegraph office and cable both the woman's husband and her brother-in-law, the boy's father. They only have to wait until they are picked up."

"But it is too late in the day. His dad won't be able to get here tonight. Where will they sleep?"

"Ellis Island was built to accommodate detained immigrants. A bed has been allotted for them to share in the woman's dormitory."

The Fairies tapped each child on each elbow, transporting them to the women's dormitory. By day, this long room on the third floor that slept 300 women, overlooking the huge Registry Room, was another waiting area. But at night, hundreds of bunk beds were dropped from the ceiling and suspended in rows of three hammock-like beds stacked one on top of the other.

Like most evenings during this peak immigration period, tonight the room was jam-packed. Women and children sat, lay or hung over most of the beds. The noise level was only a little lower than the din in the Grand Hall. The women and children not huddled on beds stood off to the side in small groups, talking.

"This looks a bit intimidating," said Bennett.

"Yes," said Abigail, "I would be afraid to sleep."

"Oh dear, if you find THIS intimidating, I had better cross the visit to the men's dormitory off our tour," fretted Alicia.

"You would feel a little better if your aunt or your mother were with you to take care of you," reassured Enjella.

"Well," said Abigail, a frown of doubt squishing her eyebrows. "May-ay-be."

"During the day, the three-tiered beds are tied back up to the ceiling and this room functions as a waiting room," Enjella informed them.

"Boy, they moved thousands of people through here! It is just amazing," said Abigail.

"But wait, you said this would be fun. What is fun about this?" asked Bennett.

"Look over there at young Tom McGlew," said Alicia.

"What happened to his jacket with his note and his tags?" asked Abigail.

"Why is he all wet? Where did he come from?" asked Bennett.

"The men's bathroom. He just had his first shower," said Alicia. Pop! A towel wrapped turban style around her hair and her wings dripped copious amounts of water.

"What do you mean 'first'?" both Bennett and Abigail asked, their voices squeaking with surprise.

"In Ireland he only bathed in tubs of water, less than once a week," said Alicia. Pop! A metal tub appeared over her head with a little yellow rubber duck swimming in it.

"Pee-EWWW!" said Abigail, holding her nose.

"I still don't see what is so much fun about a shower," said Bennett.

"Listen!" commanded Enjella. Pop! A captain's hat appeared on her head. They all flew in a little closer.

"Aunt Eileen, you wouldn't believe it!" Ten-year-old Tom danced in front of his aunt, and every child within listening distance turned to hear what the boy had to say.

"T'was a wee bit o' heaven! Water, cozy warm as a blanket, was pour'n, out o'the sky. Free for all to use! The soap! Oh the soap! Like rubbing on butter it was so soft. I slathered it upon meself. Not a wee bit like the lye soap a smell'n like horsetail back at home, don't ya know. There were magical bubbles everywhere. The scent was prettier than roses – smell me! I smell beautiful too!" Tom waved his arms in front of his aunt's nose.

"Aye, so you do," laughed Aunt Eileen. "By the sword o' Saint Michael, 'tis a miracle that a boy who smelled so foul as you can now smell so beau-ti-ful. America is a GRAND country, don't ya know."

"Aunt Eileen you have to have a go at it! The room is toasty warm and steamy. There's buckets and buckets o'water just free fer the takin'. It just keeps coming out of the sky. It was pouring down on top o'me head. It was dripping down me ears. It was warming my shoulders. It was a wee bit o' heaven. And now I am sparkling clean!"

Aunt Eileen threw back her head and laughed, which brought a smile to the faces of the women around her. All the children listening started smiling too. They tugged their mother's skirts and sleeves; they wanted to try the shower too.

The History Explorers laughed. Alicia waved her wand. She filled the air with soapsuds and they tumbled through the bubbles, soaking in the boy's happiness.

"Well, he certainly does not need our help," said Abigail, after a final somersault of joy. "Bring us to someone who does."

ZAAAAAP! The wands glimmered and a spark flew.

"WHEN are we?" both Abigail and Bennett asked at the same time.

Pop! Trumpets blared over Alicia's head. She blew a loud note through the one in her hand. Alicia lowered her horn and announced; "Now we are in 1910."

"The clothes do not look much different," Abigail observed.

Bennett looked down at a young woman wearing peasant garb; a dark dress with a colorful apron and shawl. She was staring at her hands, wringing her handkerchief, in front of an inspector's desk. She had an "L" chalk marked on her coat. Bennett spoke aloud what the Time Travelers were all thinking to themselves, "What can we do to help this young woman? What's the problem?"

The Fairy tour group zoomed down to the inspector's desk. The young woman stood hunched over and silent, with a stony white face, looking close to tears.

"Translator!" boomed the inspector. Almost instantly, a young gentleman appeared at his side.

"Who is that?" whispered Bennett.

"The young Fiorello LaGuardia," said Enjella with a smile. Pop! Alicia and Enjella were wearing red, white and blue striped outfits and American flags were flying in their hair.

Bennett and Abigail looked at each other, with blank looks on their faces. Perplexed, Bennett shrugged and turned to the Fairies. "We give up, who is that?"

"Haven't you ever heard of LaGuardia Airport?" said Alicia, the flags now drooping down and hanging limp around little poles.

"Well, sure, it's an airport in New York City, but that doesn't give us any clue as to who LaGuardia is," said Abigail.

"Right now he is a law student at night, supporting himself by working as a translator during the day here at Ellis Island. Because LaGuardia was the son of Italian immigrants who came through Ellis Island many years ago, he is very sympathetic to the troubles of the immigrants and dedicated to helping them through processing at Ellis Island. From nine o'clock in the morning until seven o'clock at night, he is here seven days a week, making it his job to help everyone he can."

"He must have been a really good translator if they named an airport after him!" said Bennett.

"Well he was, but it is not for his work at Ellis Island that his name is still famous. Later in life, LaGuardia becomes the Mayor of New York City," said Enjella.

Their attention was arrested by the fact that the lady at the desk began to weep into her twisted handkerchief and Mr. LaGuardia looked upset. They listened more closely.

"If YOU cannot figure out what she is saying, I don't know what we can do with her!" exclaimed the inspector. "Here we have yet another person without papers coming in from Northern Italy."

Mr. LaGuardia replied to the inspector. "The difficulty here is that there are too many Italian dialects. Golly! The Italian government hasn't even decided which one should be the Official National Language yet.

With such a strange accent, even if the base word would be similar, it is nigh impossible to communicate with her."

"This girl has failed to answer a single question. We have no method to corroborate the veracity of the information concerning this unattended female with no known employable skills and unconfirmed connections in this country. If she could communicate, we could ask her about her impaired locomotion." The inspector sighed. "Her medical papers are not complete. She has not yet been given a comprehensive medical examination."

"You told us 'L' is for lame," said Abigail. "She must have been walking funny when she climbed the initial stairway, during the preliminary exam."

The inspector waved his hand and instructed LaGuardia. "Take her to the medical inspectors on the third floor. I do not have any more time to figure out what she is trying to say."

"But we can understand her!" cried Abigail.

"I will continue to endeavor to communicate with her," said LaGuardia, gently taking the woman's elbow, and turning her away from the desk as she continued to cry.

"That's why they need us, and our magic translation spell," said Enjella.

"She is telling them that she is supposed to meet her fiancé here," Abigail continued. "He is waiting for word from her. He is supposed to come to pick her up."

"Isn't that one of the twenty-nine questions on the ship's manifest?" Bennett asked Enjella. "Shouldn't the officials already know the immigrant's answers? How can we tell them?"

"Let me think about it while we follow them upstairs."

The woman, tears silently streaming down her cheeks, gently escorted by Mr. LaGuardia, walked past the Stairs of Separation and climbed the stairs to the third floor examination rooms.

"I am going to whisper in the girl's ear and tell her where they are going," announced Abigail.

Enjella smiled a small smile. "That is why we are here; not necessarily to change the course of history, but to facilitate it!"

Bennett and Abigail looked confused. "Make it easier?"

"Yes. We must ensure this young lady's safe entry into the country. AND it certainly would not hurt if along the way we could make it less stressful and less heart-wrenching for the immigrants to endure this process."

Abigail zipped up to the girl and whispered into her ear. The rest the group saw her buzzing around and stabbing at the air as she flapped her wings and talked.

The girl stopped crying. Abigail buzzed back to the group. They watched the girl and Mr. LaGuardia climb the stairs. The girl seemed more composed.

"Her shoe is broken!" said Abigail to Bennett. "I saw it when she leaned over. Maybe that is why she is limping."

Bennett flew over to Mr. LaGuardia and whispered in his ear. LaGuardia was still experimenting with different pronunciations of basic Italian words to try to get the woman to understand what was happening.

"Are you perhaps meeting your fiancé here?" Mr. LaGuardia said to the woman he was escorting up the stairs. "Can we help you contact someone while you are being processed? We cannot release you, as a single woman. We must turn you over to your relations. Do you have any relatives in the States?"

"Basta, Basta, Non," the woman muttered over and over. Abigail could see tears beginning to form again in the corners of her eyes.

Abigail whispered one more time into the woman's ear.

Bennett started whispering in Mr. LaGuardia's ear.

With the help of Fairy magic, Mr. LaGuardia understood that the woman had no relatives here, but her fiancé had come over to the United States two years ago and finally saved enough money to send for her. The girl now understood the procedures that had to be followed; and at the top of the stairs, she pointed to her shoe.

LaGuardia saw that her shoe was broken and smiled to encourage her. He advised her in Italian that he would send a telegram to her fiancé to have him come to meet her at the island. She must submit to a full examination so the officials could see if she was healthy enough to be admitted to the country.

The girl did not seem to understand what he said; she still looked confused and uncertain at his words. She caught her lip with her teeth, but shook her head yes.

"If she is not healthy," warned Alicia, "she will be deported!"

"And her poor fiancé will have to go away without her?" Bennett muttered to himself.

"If she is healthy in mind and body Mr. LaGuardia will escort them both to City Hall in Manhattan where they will be married immediately. Then she will be able to start her life in America."

"Body AND mind?" said Bennett. "How do they judge the 'mind' part?"

"It is not an exact science," said Alicia. Pop! Rulers dangled from her ears. "Not now, and certainly not then. Sometimes just wearing a grim face and not reacting or showing emotion during the process made officials think an immigrant was mentally ill."

"That is horrible. What if the person was afraid of the official?"

"Good question Bennett," said Alicia. Pop! Bells started ringing. "Many people left their old countries for that very reason: they were afraid of their government's officials. They were stopped on their streets for no reason. Their homes were searched without warrant. They could be randomly questioned and detained. All these things are illegal in the United States. But the immigrants don't know what to expect here and when frightened they could have trained themselves to not react."

Bennett scratched his head. "That's even worse than I thought. I was just thinking a person could believe it was more dignified not to act upset or react to the process. Boy, everything you did put your future in this country in jeopardy, including staying composed!"

"Sadly, yes," said Enjella.

"This is agony!" said Abigail, "how long will this all take? Is there something else we can do to help? I won't be able to stand the suspense!

The poor lady – how intimidating it must feel to have to have a medical exam in a place where you can't understand anyone! And what if she acts too passively and they think she is mentally ill?"

"Here's what we can do to ensure your future and hers," said Enjella. "Abigail, you tell her to have courage. She has to try to communicate that she is smart, capable, and can be financially responsible, in spite of not speaking the language. She must trust that Mr. LaGuardia and the rest of the staff at Ellis Island will do the best they can for her."

"I got it!" Abigail announced. "I can tell her to show the officials her broken shoes. Then she could take them off and walk perfectly well."

"That's right," said Bennett. "Then the officials would know that she is smart enough to figure out what is going on, in spite of not speaking the language."

"Done," cried Abigail. She winged right over to the anxious looking woman and whispered again. After a minute or two, the woman sighed and relaxed a bit. A look of determination came over her face. She stood up straight, forced a smile, and limped into the examination room. The only sign left of her agitation was the way she continued to twist her handkerchief in her hands.

"Now we just have to sit here and wait?" complained Bennett.

"Wait? Why would Fairies wait when they have magical command of the passage of time?" teased Alicia.

"I understand your anxiety," said Enjella, "and your impatience at the delay. You are experiencing what many of the immigrants felt. The waiting was the hardest part! But we won't torture you."

Simultaneously, the Fairies touched the children on their elbows and twisted time.

"It is now two days later," announced Enjella.

The History Explorers were at the top of the Stairs of Separation. A beaming Mr. LaGuardia and the shyly smiling woman came toward them, and walked down the left side. From there they went toward a waiting room where a blushing young man with very big ears stood, twisting his hat in his hands. The woman turned pink and offered her hand to the waiting man, who took it with another blush of his own. A halting conversation started between the man and Mr. LaGuardia; the man stammered and shifted from foot to foot, big ears bright red with nervousness. The big-eared man said something to the woman, and they all began to walk toward the exit.

"What did we just see?" asked Bennett.

"The left side of the stairs leads to the outside path to the ferry building and admittance to America! The right side leads to the train ticketing office for those starting their new American life in the west, north and south of the city. The middle stairs leads to the detention rooms, either for further examination or deportation back to the old country.

"They went down the left side!" shouted Abigail. "She passed the examinations. She gets to marry her fiancé. But wait, why do they have to go to city hall to get married right now?"

"A bit more of the unequal treatment of woman, I am sorry to report," said Enjella. "The government was afraid that the man might change his mind. The jilted woman might be left destitute, with no rights, with no skills, no job and nowhere to live."

"I guess, at least if she was married, even if she later got divorced, that would give her some rights," speculated Abigail.

"Correct; although it would not be easy to get a divorce in that era."

Bennett snapped his fingers. "We can't change that system now. Cheer up! One of our ancestors passed her medical exam. She can stay in the United States!"

Pop! Party hats appeared on everyone's heads. Confetti came down from the air and noisemakers blared. Pop! A large bottle of Champagne appeared in the air, uncorked itself and began to fizz.

"Yay! Another successful processing completed, thanks to the care and efforts of the inspectors," said Bennett.

"Good job Mr. LaGuardia," said Abigail.

CHAPTER SEVEN

Separated!

Enjella winked at Alicia and twisted time again.

The confetti and hats disappeared.

Suddenly everything looked different. Bennett blinked. "Am I crazy, or did the metal fences that lined the rows just disappear?"

"They did," said Abigail. "And the walls are a brighter color and there are pictures on them."

"It's magic!" said Alicia, and punctuated her comment with one of her cartwheels.

"Not helpful," frowned Bennett.

Enjella gave Bennett a hug, "We moved time again. It is now four years later."

"I think I have whiplash from changing time so quickly," said Bennett rubbing his neck.

Alicia giggled and zapped a funny motorized back massage gizmo into the air that flew over to Bennett and began rubbing his neck.

"OOOOooo! Warmth and massage in the same ingenious device!" he giggled. "And it tickles."

Enjella glared at them and the magic massager disappeared. "As I was saying: President Theodore Roosevelt visited Ellis Island in the first year of his presidency to see the problems of immigration first hand. He made Ellis Island a special focus of his attention to ensure that immigrants were processed according to federal standards. President Roosevelt appointed a new commissioner in 1903, William Williams who began making reforms. Mr. Williams posted the new mission statement: Every immigrant must be treated with kindness and civility; neither harsh language nor rough handling will be tolerated.

"After William's second stint as commissioner, Frederic C. Howe took over at Ellis Island. He had a whole new philosophy; where Williams made the process as efficient as possible, Commissioner Howe was determined to make this a friendlier, more welcoming place."

"By the way Bennett. That was VERY observant!" laughed Alicia. Pop! A big cartoon hand appeared over his head and patted him three times. "One of the first things Howe did was to take down what came to be called 'the cages' and replace them with benches for the weary travelers to rest while they waited for their number on the manifest to be called."

Enjella picked up the narrative. "Commissioner Howe continued the improvements Williams made to the ordering and maintenance systems. Williams banished suppliers that were corrupt. Howe re-trained the workers to be more understanding and friendly. Howe adopted the motto: "that every man and woman who passes through this port may be… impressed with America's spirit of democracy."

The children's elbows were tapped again and they found themselves outside on the top of the building.

"Wow. It's scary up here."

"Sure, right here in front of the machines it is. There is no way to make all the equipment needed to run this place and the water tower look nicer. But look over there."

Once again the children were magically transported through space, in an instant. They found themselves in a lovely rooftop garden where children were running, riding in wagons and playing games. Adults, smiling and strolling, turned their faces toward the sun.

"Who are these children? Why are these people up here?"

"They are waiting. Either to be met by someone to take them to their new home, or for their entry issues to be resolved, or for a sick member of their family to be released from the hospital."

"Oh no, there are so many problems," Abigail said with a sad smile, and Bennett shook his head with sympathy.

"Yes, this was a difficult business. The staff here tried their best to efficiently process the many people flooding into the country. Howe turned the lawns into playgrounds to try to ease the hardship of being detained. Administrators and staff worked hard to be courteous to the immigrants throughout the process," said Alicia.

ZAP! The Time Travelers were once again back in the noisy Grand Hall. Abigail put her hands over her ears. It was an involuntary reaction to the loud racket.

"This is June 1914. In two months, the Great War will erupt in Europe. The Continent is already in turmoil: economies are faltering and people have no jobs. Desperate for work, a better way of life and sometimes even for enough food to eat, people are streaming into the United States," explained Enjella.

Alicia added, "This fueled a great democratic debate: how many people should be allowed into our country, and from what places."

Bennett said, "Our country is still discussing that today."

The noise in the room suddenly grew louder. The babble of voices turned into a roar.

"It is just chaos in here!" Abigail exclaimed.

"No wonder people lost their patience," said Bennett. "It must have been hard for the staff to deal with all this noise and all these people, day after day."

Right at Abigail's elbow, an eleven-year-old red haired girl burst into tears. "I won't go without me Mother!" she shouted, and grabbed on to her mother's skirt wildly.

"Why are they trying to take THIS girl away?" wondered Abigail.

"I'm afraid you must, little girl," an inspector said firmly, "your eyes are not healthy and we must make sure you are not bringing any diseases into the country. Your mother must stay in the line with your aunt and the other children until she completes the legal inspection. She will find you when she is through." He pulled the little girl away.

She sobbed as the inspector handed her to a Matron who took her hand and guided her toward the stairs. Her mother called to her, "I will find you, Love."

"Ohhhhhh, this is horrible," said Abigail. "Where are they going?"

"To the new infirmary. Anyone sick with a potentially contagious disease was quarantined until the authorities were sure they were not contagious," Enjella explained.

"I am going to fly along with them to make sure she is ok. This is horrible!" repeated Abigail.

"It is," agreed Enjella, "but believe it or not, this is an improvement over how contagious diseases used to be handled."

Enjella and Abigail took off after the Matron, who hurried away pulling the still sobbing girl by the hand. The Matron was also carrying a crying toddler. The small sad group walked past the legal inspectors' desks to the Stairs of Separation at the far side of the Grand Hall and walked down the middle stairs. The Irish girl and the baby continued to cry. Abigail felt so sorry for the slender girl.

She must be so frightened, Abigail worried. "Does she have trachoma?"

Enjella replied, "Perhaps. It is too early to tell. She will be quarantined in the contagious disease ward for the duration of the disease incubation period."

Abigail looked confused.

Enjella explained further, "The girl will be kept under observation to see if she shows any symptoms of the disease. The test for trachoma takes ten days. But these eye conditions could also be symptoms of other contagious diseases."

The trio, trailed overhead by the invisible flying Fairy and friend, continued their descent down the middle of the Stairs of Separation. Proceeding out of the building toward the dock, they took a right and walked down a grassy corridor to a side pier. The Matron said something to a man in a small boat. The Matron, the crying baby and the noiselessly weeping girl got into the boat and sailed away!

CHAPTER EIGHT

Landing in the Hospital

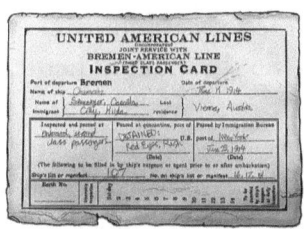

"Where are they taking her? Did they tell her mother what disease she has? Does her mother know what's happening?" Abigail was so upset she stopped, midair, her hair standing up with worry.

"Cool!" said Bennett, materializing by her side. "The Fairy magic is making your hair express your feelings, just like Alicia!" Alicia popped out of the air next to Abigail and took a bow.

"Is that a GOOD thing?" Abigail demanded. Alicia frowned.

"Whatever!!!" Abigail stamped her foot in the air. "Will they take her away from her mother permanently? Are they shipping her back to Ireland?"

"No, the hospital wards for contagious diseases are separated from the main processing building by a lagoon. The boat is delivering the sick children to the ward. Medical experts at that time were just beginning to understand how disease spreads. The building designers thought water dividing the wards would help contain germs.

"Do you want to fly over there?" asked Enjella, "or should we just pop into the contagious disease ward?"

Before they could decide, Alicia mischievously ZAAAAPED them back into the Registry Room on the second floor.

"Hey what did you do THAT for?" demanded Bennett.

"Yeah, what?" said Enjella, with her hands on her hips.

"There is something we want you to see here. Enjella, you remember," Alicia winked with a smug smile on her face.

SHREEEEKKKK!

A loud yowl of pain momentarily stopped the noisy din in the medical line as every head turned toward the sound.

An Irish woman lay on the ground, her traveling companion bent over her, frantically trying to revive her. The children in the group were bunched together in fear.

"Is that the mother of… ?" The loud crying of a little girl in the group interrupted Bennett's question. An official came over, motioned for a medical orderly to assist, and together they revived the fainted woman. The woman swayed on her feet, her freckles standing out in stark contrast to the paleness of her skin. The orderly picked her up as if she were light as a feather and took her away.

"My goodness," said Abigail. "Another person in distress. I see she has a chalk mark on her jacket but I could not read the letter."

"What is wrong? Where are they taking HER?" asked Bennett.

The History Explorers flew down to hear better.

"… to the maternity ward," said the official to the remaining distraught Irish woman standing with the children. The woman's shoulders sagged and she put a shaky hand to her forehead. The children all burst into tears.

"First sissy, now mother!" cried one of the little girls, tugging on the woman's skirt.

The official put a kind hand on the woman's arm. "Don't you worry none, miss. Our maternity ward may be extremely busy, but it is the finest in the land. She would not get better care anywhere in the world. Why it is a fine stroke of luck that she arrive here, where her confinement can be overseen properly."

The woman took heart at his kindness, blew her nose in her handkerchief, picked up all the bags that were scattered about her, and marshaled the four children together. The oldest girl, who could not have been more than nine, picked up the remaining bag and the smallest boy's hand and they all fell back into the line.

"They are so brave," whispered Abigail.

"Geez!" said Bennett, "it seems like every person in line has an incredible story. And look at how many of them there are."

"That's what I've been trying to tell you," said Alicia. Pop! A colorful bunch of balloons appeared over her head, and tied themselves to her hair. Alicia started to rise to the rafters. Suddenly the balloons broke free and floated up to the ceiling where they disappeared.

Enjella cleared her throat. "If you are quite finished?" she asked Alicia.

"Quite," said Alicia, floating back down with a very satisfied look on her face.

"We are here to experience the stories of these immigrants," said Enjella.

"Speak for yourself!" stated Alicia. "I'm here for the drama!"

Bennett and Abigail smiled. "We know how much you love drama!" said Bennett.

"Up until now we have been following the immigrants as they made their way through the process," announced tour-guide Alicia. Pop! She was all decked out in a stewardess uniform, a hat at a rakish angle on her head. She waved a flashlight, as if directing everyone to the exit. "Now we begin the second half of our journey. We will pay attention to the stories of just two of the passengers in 1914, two young girls."

"Did you forget about that Irish girl?" asked Enjella at exactly the same time that Abigail said, "What about the girl we were following? Is it her story we are here to witness? What is happening to her?"

ZAP! The History Explorers were back out on top of the awning over the grand entrance, watching the boat disappear.

"Gotta love that time bending function of this new wand," smiled Alicia, flexing her wand. "Isn't technology great?"

Abigail's hand flew to her mouth, "Did we miss anything? Are they still taking the girl to the hospital?"

"Yes! How do we want to follow?" asked Enjella again.

"I want the full experience," said Bennett. "Let's fly right behind that poor Irish girl as if we had to go through everything that she is living through."

The Time Travelers zoomed over the lagoon and out towards the open harbor. They soon caught up with the small boat. The boat pulled around the peninsula that contained the main building of the hospital and into the next lagoon. The Irish girl had stopped sobbing and was looking at the sun sparkling on the water, a forlorn expression and a single tear remaining on her face.

The boat containing the Matron and her two charges docked on Island Three, in front of one of the pavilions of the Contagious Disease Wards. The History Explorers circled overhead. The trio was handed out of the boat. The Matron, still carrying the baby, walked into the building, holding the frightened girl's hand.

The gloomy light inside the doorway matched everyone's mood.

"What is her name?" whispered Abigail to Enjella.

"Kate," was the reply.

The Fairies' group hovered in the air and in suspense. A doctor was called. He examined Kate's eyes, looked in her ears and took out his stethoscope. And still they waited. The exam was completed, but then there was paperwork to be done.

A decision was reached.

The Matron marched Kate up the stairs and into a long room filled with hospital beds. The rows and rows of beds seemed like they never ended.

"How many beds are in this room?" whispered Bennett.

"Are all these kids contagious?" whispered Abigail.

"It is not pretty," acknowledged Enjella. "These poor kids are sick, in a strange new country, and they are quarantined so they can't see their family members. Plus some of them don't speak the language. There are a lot of unhappy, frightened children here."

The Irish girl was undressed and put in a bed next to another little girl, roughly the same age. She looked very upset at parting with her clothing. The nurses took it away without a word.

"Where are they taking her clothes?" asked Abigail.

"To the huge laundry room where they clean and sterilize clothes and bed sheets," explained Enjella.

"Don't worry!" laughed Alicia. "They will bring them back, nice and clean."

"This is the measles ward," advised Enjella.

"Itchy Ishcabibble! Look at the girl next to Kate. She has horrible red splotches all over her face and arms," said Bennett.

"You should see how bad they are on her stomach," said Alicia with a sympathetic chuckle.

"I bet those itch like crazy," said Bennett, unconsciously scratching his arm.

"That girl is Hilda. She just arrived three days ago on the ship named CHEMNITZ, which left from Bremen, Germany. She was born in Vienna, Austria. Ooo! It looks like she celebrated her twelfth birthday on the ship during the transatlantic journey," Alicia read off a clipboard that magically appeared in her hand. "According to the manifest, Hilda is accompanied by her mother and her sister and traveled second class to join her father who had already immigrated several years ago."

"Wait," said Bennett. "I thought you said that first and second class passengers did not have to go through Ellis Island, they were processed on board their ship."

Pop! A fanfare sounded and a graduation cap appeared on his head. Hands materialized and patted him on the back and on his head. More balloons appeared and floated up to the rafters. "It never gets old!" chortled Alicia. "Congrats for paying attention! But think: what is the exception to that rule?"

"Ah, yes, I remember," said Bennett. "People who failed the health inspection or did not answer the immigration questions to the satisfaction of the inspector still had to come over to Ellis Island for further questioning."

"Correct again!" shouted Alicia. Pop! More confetti streamed out of thin air above Bennett's head.

"It's still not getting old," she shouted, catching pieces of confetti with one hand, and throwing them up again, and tossing streamers with the other.

"It's getting a bit old for me," said Enjella, hands on her hips, turning a stern glare at Alicia.

"Sometimes you are no fun, Enjella," said Alicia.

"Some of us have work to do here," Enjella said firmly.

"True," said Alicia. "Poor Hilda Schweiger seems to have been exposed to measles on the voyage over here. By the time she pulled into port this week, her eyes were glassy and there were some tiny bumps on the backs of her ears. The health inspector aboard the ship sent her right here to Ellis Island's new contagious ward. By this afternoon the red spots appeared over most of her body," said Alicia, big red spots sprouting on her face.

Enjella said, "This is state-of-the-art hospital. The main hospital was just renovated to provide care for immigrants with non-transmittable diseases. These contagious disease wards were completed in 1908, but lack of funding and building issues kept patients from using them until 1911."

"Wow! Everything here is brand new and sparkling clean. The good old U.S. of A. is taking good care of the immigrants." Bennett whistled with appreciation.

"Well sure," Alicia said, "The people of the United States did want to help these poor sick immigrants. But there was another, more selfish reason to allocate the funds from taxpayer money and construct this great hospital: people did not want immigrants with contagious diseases brought to the main hospitals in New York potentially spreading the diseases."

Bennett and Abigail looked a little sad.

"Cheer up," said Alicia. Pop! Sparklers lit up in her hair, shooting colorful little sparks of light. "It is human nature to want to protect yourselves. The good news is that the doctors and nurses provided excellent care here. Most of the people who were lucky enough to have their diseases detected by the inspectors got cured in this hospital. Very few died, and even fewer were deported for having an incurable disease. Quarantining them, even though emotionally hard on the patients and their families waiting for them, actually was a good thing, preventing the spreading of the disease to the families of the infected as well as to the rest of America."

The children simply looked at each other. They had just been given an overwhelming amount of information; they were silent trying to process it.

"Let us resume our mission," said Enjella.

She cleared her throat and referred to her clipboard. "We know that Kate's family is still being processed. Now we will look at Hilda's family."

ZAAAAAAP!

The Time Travelers were suddenly on a balcony overlooking one of the waiting areas in the registry building. A middle-aged man removed his cap and began talking to the inspector. A middle-aged woman and a young woman stood at the inspector's side. Both women looked with smiling faces at the cap-less man.

"Hilda's father met the CHEMNITZ when it docked, only to find that his family had been taken here," said Enjella.

"SHHHHhhh!" whispered Alicia, finger up to her mouth. Pop! 'Shush' signs appeared on her hair. "We don't want to miss the live action!"

"… one of you will have to stay here until the case of the measles is resolved," the inspector advised.

The man looked very upset.

"Resolved? Is my little girl very sick?" asked the man, turning his cap over and over in his hands. The inspector did not say anything, he just looked down at his papers. The two ladies' faces clouded back over with worry and fear.

Everyone was silent. The inspector restated his directive. "You may choose whether you stay to wait for your sick daughter or whether you leave your wife and daughter to wait."

"I am unsure what to do," the man muttered looking helplessly at his wife. He launched into a long speech in German which the History Explorers heard as: "I cannot stay to wait for our little one, my business is new and will not run itself. Just to come today I had to hire a man to run the store and I will lose my whole day's profits to pay his wages. And to leave you! How can this be? I need you both to work with me right away. These are precarious days. There are many things required if our delicatessen is to succeed. We must protect our investment in rent and equipment. I have waited many months for you to arrive. I fear I cannot spare you another day, let alone two weeks. And to leave you here alone! To do what, fritter the time away while you worry about our little girl? What can be done?"

"Rudolf, I have been discussing our situation with a woman from the Leo House," said Caecilia Schweiger, the middle aged women.

Mr. Rudolf Schweiger looked surprised, "You discuss our family with strangers?" he questioned.

"Difficult situations call for difficult choices," said Caecilia firmly. "The Leo House is an organization dedicated to helping Germanic people with the immigration process. The Sisters of Saint Agnes know how to help us. They have translated the procedures for me. The Sister counsels that our daughter will be receiving wonderful care at the hospital, so there is no benefit to any of us staying here. We can do nothing more here for our darling Hilda.

"What we CAN do is post a bond to ensure our return for our little girl when she is well. The Sisters at the Leo House have a program for sponsoring immigrants. They will help us by advancing the necessary funds."

"No charity! I will not take charity," Rudolf protested, his hands out before him, waving her away.

"It is not charity, it is a loan. We must put up collateral. This loan ensures you will not lose any days of work. Furthermore, Cilly and I can begin immediately to work to help you with the grand opening. This is our only hope. Our only way to remedy our situation."

A nun dressed in a black habit rushed over to the group. "Here you are Caecilia," said the nun, speaking in German too. "I have brought the necessary paperwork, so we can begin the process…"

ZZZZzzzaaaaP! Alicia's wand whipped out and back so quickly it seemed to land on both children's elbows simultaneously.

The Time Travelers materialized in the rafters of the huge Measles Ward A room. They looked down on the center aisle of beds, Bennett facing the beds on one wall, and Abigail looking at the rows of beds on the other.

Bennett and Abigail just floated, blinking for a minute.

Enjella spoke. "Unlike Kate, whose family is forced to remain in the dormitories on the third floor of the big administrative building, Hilda's mother and sister are free to go with her father. But only because Mrs. Schweiger, with the help of the German Immigration Aide Society, the Leo House, was able to post a $250 bond to ensure that they would come back to pick Hilda up when she recovers in two weeks or so."

Abigail scratched her head. "What is a BOND anyway?"

Pop! A huge dictionary appeared in Alicia's hand. She opened the leather-bound book and read, "A sum of money used to secure the return of someone; usually money posted by a person accused of a crime to ensure they will return for the trial date."

"But Hilda is not a criminal!" said Abigail.

"No she is not," said Bennett, "and $250 was a fortune at that time! The dollar amount in 1914 is worth about twenty-two times that amount today, when you account for inflation." He stopped to do the math. "Ishkabibble! That would be five THOUSAND, five hundred dollars! Mr. Schweiger must be very worried about having to find collateral for the loan of the bond money."

Enjella nodded, with a serious expression on her face. "Yes, they would have had to promise a piece of expensive business equipment as a guarantee to the Leo House to insure their return, their payment of medical expenses and the return of the bond money to the Sisters."

"What if they could not have afforded it? I mean what if the Aide society could not help them?" demanded Abigail. "What would have happened then?"

"Then one of the parents would have had to stay here to wait while Hilda recovered," answered Enjella, "just like Kate's family."

"We don't even want to think about the poor people whose family members died in the hospitals," said Alicia sadly. The whole group grew sad and silent. All their wings drooped at the same time and they drifted down to the ground, heartbroken at all the sadness that transpired in this place.

"This will never do," said Enjella, reenergizing everyone's wings with a touch of her wand.

"That's right," said Alicia. "These girls have what the United States Public Health Service called a "Class A condition". Even though it is contagious and the Immigration Service will not allow them to enter the country, it is a short-term disease that is curable. They will be provided the best medical care, and chances are, their families will even get help paying the medical bill."

"Yes," Enjella chimed in, "Whether solely for humanitarian reasons, or mostly for practical ones, the government decided that people who wanted to become citizens and caught these diseases onboard the ship during their passage should be granted treatment, regardless of their ability to pay."

Alicia jumped up in the air. "Everyone in this ward will receive medical treatment until they are cured. So let's perk up our helping wings. We are going to try to make life better for everyone we can possibly help here!"

They were directly over the heads of Kate and Hilda. The two little girls were now side-by-side with empty beds on either side of them. The few other children in the room were far down the on the other side near the nurses' desk. The beds in the middle aisle of the room were empty. Both girls looked miserable. Abigail pointed, and they all saw a single large tear slide slowly down Kate's now red and splotchy face.

"I guess Kate has the measles for sure, since she is in the measles ward," said Bennett.

"Another brilliant deduction by our own Sherlock Holmes," said Alicia. Pop! Her old Sherlock Holmes hat perched at a jaunty angle on her head.

"Gee," said Abigail, "you don't have to be sarcastic. It is hard to keep up with all the zapping back and forth that we are doing."

The Fairies' group sat down on the rafters and looked glum. Sympathetic spots appeared on Enjella and Abigail's forehead.

"Hey, I hope you are not sick!" said Bennett to Abigail.

"Not to worry. We can't catch anything," said Enjella with a pat on Abigail's head. "First of all, I know you both have had your vaccinations.

Measles has been effectively wiped out in the United States today because everyone gets vaccinated. And secondly, Fairy magic, time travel and all that good mumbo jumbo will protect you," said Alicia and she punctuated her remark with a hearty thump on Bennett's back.

"What can we do to help these girls?" fretted Abigail.

"The best thing for them right now is sleep," said Enjella.

"They are probably too frightened and upset to sleep," said Bennett.

"I know I would be," agreed Abigail. "Maybe we can sing them a lullaby, the way you used to do for us, Enjella."

"Or wait!" said Bennett. "Can't you use your sleep spell to lull them to sleep, or your magic dream spell, to make them have a good dream?"

"TOOT-toot!" Alicia blew a whistle so hard, the police cap that had POPPED onto her head blew straight up into the air, flipped over, and plopped back down.

"I already told you this during our last adventure," Enjella put her hands on her hips. Alicia adjusted her cap with her white-gloved hand, and hung the whistle around her neck. "We cannot use our magic directly on people from the past – or else we could change history too much. All we can do is use our magic around them, or on ourselves, so we can better help them."

"Tricky," said Bennett. "So we will have to be trickier! What do they need the most?" he asked.

"They need to stop worrying," said Abigail. "But how can we help them do that? They are all alone, they are in a strange place, they are sick, they have a contagious disease, they don't know what is happening to them and they don't know where their parents and siblings are!"

"That just about sums it up," said Alicia. Pop! She dashed some chalk in a line under a tall column of numbers on a chalkboard suspended in midair, wrote a big number and spun around to face them.

"This is not going to get fixed quickly either," cautioned Enjella. "In the best case scenario the disease will take two weeks to run its course while the doctors and nurses apply all the best remedies they knew in 1914."

"We should explain to them what is going on, so they won't be so afraid," said Abigail.

"THEN we can sing them a lullaby," said Bennett.

"That is a good place to start," said Enjella. "What are you going to say?"

The two children sporting fairy wings looked at each other. "I guess for right now," Bennett said slowly, "we should just tell them that this is a hospital, they have the measles, their families are ok, and they don't need to be worried. We should also explain that the best thing...no! the ONLY thing they should do now is try to get some rest."

"Yes," agreed Abigail, "the more they rest, the sooner they will get better and the sooner they will be reunited with their families." Suddenly she looked very upset as a new thought occurred to her. "They both WILL get better, won't they?"

"Well, you are here today right? So they do make it," said Enjella.

"Not so fast," said the urchin Alicia. "Once you time travel you CAN affect the outcome of certain events. We aim to carefully affect events for the better, but once you start messing with time..." Alicia shook her head warningly.

"I don't want to be here if we could make things worse!" said Abigail nervously.

Alicia winked mischievously, "But what if we were not the only time travelers, and someone else was messing things up as we speak, so it is our jobs to make sure the real events happen as they should?"

"Ouch!" said Bennett. "My head hurts!"

Enjella held up her hand, "Basta! Back to the original question: will the girls survive the measles? Once the new contagious wards were up and running on Ellis Island the fatality rate from the measles dropped to almost zero. It was a far cry from the days when there was no hospital at Ellis Island, and the sick immigrants were sent to Swinburne Island."

Alicia continued the explanation. "Yes, before this great hospital with all of its modern equipment, like X-ray machines and like autoclaves to sterilize instruments, sick immigrants were at first sent to a New York City hospital. But several city-wide epidemics broke out because of the diseases the immigrants carried. The city tried to solve this problem by sending contagious immigrants, including children, all by themselves to dormitories on Swinburne Island. Their families, or anyone traveling with them suspected of having a contagious disease, even if they did not yet have symptoms, were quarantined on a different island, called Hoffman's Island until the incubation period for the suspected disease was over. The care there was not the best and the diseases continued to spread; families even caught them while in quarantine."

"Both these girls are very sick and need a great deal of care to survive this. But at the Ellis Island hospital they will be given the best care available in 1914, in a clean and sterile environment. Since they are still contagious for the first four days after the rash breaks out…" said Enjella.

"I guess that explains the sign," Bennett pointed. A sign posted right near the nurse's station read:

NO HUGGING OR
KISSING THE CHILDREN

"That is horrible!" said Abigail. "So no one will help them?"

"Well that IS the policy, and the nurses do have to be careful not to catch the diseases themselves, but most of the health care workers are very conscientious, germ conscious and dedicated to helping the sick. They not only do their jobs very well, but they try to be caring and compassionate. Oh! Look!"

An imposing woman in a white, crisply starched uniform with a perky hat walked in between the beds of the two girls. She took their temperatures, one at a time, cleansing the instrument carefully in between. She pulled the cool sheets around each girl and smoothed their pillows after she took each pulse. She smiled briefly.

"That is Nurse Jennie Colligan," Alicia introduced. Pop! A big heart appeared over her head, decorated with lace and bows. A line appeared down the middle and the heart opened. Pop! Another heart popped out and that one opened too, revealing little pinkfoil-wrapped chocolate candies that spilled out of the heart and fell into Bennett and Abigail's open hands.

Enjella continued while the children ate the delicious candy. "A kindhearted woman, Nurse Colligan lived and worked here with the other nurses for over ten years. She showed tenderness and love and took such good care of the sick children everyone called her 'Mother' Colligan."

Down below the munching children, Mother Colligan whispered, "Hello little loves! I will be sure 'n take good care of ye. For now just rest, don't be troubling your heads with anything."

Both girls seemed too sick to understand what she said. They both stared mutely at her, too intimidated and miserable to attempt to talk. Nurse Colligan squeezed each girl's shoulder with a smile, picked up the medical equipment, arranged it in its proper place on the tray and rolled it down the aisle back to her station.

Petrified with fear, neither girl moved her head. They both stared straight ahead, with heavy eyelids hanging over half-closed eyes.

"They still don't know what is going on, do they?" said Bennett.

"That is where our job comes in, we have to help them figure it out," said Alicia.

"But I don't speak German," said Abigail.

"Don't forget the power of Fairy magic," announced Alicia. Pop! A fanfare blared on sparkling brass trumpets.

Abigail flapped her wings rapidly for courage. Still invisible, she swooped down and hovered between the two girls beds.

She hesitated, and then, since she was miniature sized, she sat down on Hilda's shoulder. The girl stirred a little, but otherwise did not seem to feel her weight.

Abigail racked her brains, but she could not think of what to say. *How would the little girl be comforted by a whisper in her ear anyway?* She wondered.

Abigail closed her eyes, searching for the right words. All of a sudden she opened her mouth and began to sing:

Kommt ein Vogel geflogen,
Setzt sich neider auf mein' Fuß
Hat ein Briefchen im Schnabel,
Von der Mutter ein' Gruß

Lieber Vogel, flieg weiter,
Bring ein' Gruß mit, einen Kuß
Denn ich kann dich nicht begleiten,
Weil ich hier bleiben muß.

Bennett, anxiously hovering within earshot overhead, whispered to the Fairies, "Whoa. Where did that come from?"

The two Fairies shrugged, and for once, did not seem to have the answer.

"Wait a minute," Bennett said. "That tune sounds familiar but I never heard those words before.

Enjella laughed. "That's right, you heard it in English as:

A bird comes a-flying
It settles on my foot,
It has a letter in its beak,
A greeting from my mother.

Dear bird, fly on,
Bring a greeting with a kiss
For I cannot go with you,
Since I must stay here.

Alicia waved her magic wand, twice: once to take away the automatic translation spell and the other to wind back time approximately one and one third minutes, and Bennett again heard Abigail sing the folk song, but this time in the original Austrian dialect of German.

Bennett snapped his fingers. "Now I know where I have heard this song. My grandmother used to sing it to us."

Alicia zapped a graduation hat on Bennett's head, but at one glance from Enjella the trumpets instantly disappeared without blowing a fanfare. "Good job, Bennett," she whispered instead. Pop! The big hand that materialized out of thin air patted him on the back.

Hilda sighed when Abigail finished singing, and closed her eyes, settling into the bed. Abigail whispered, "Don't worry. Your mother did not forget about you. You are in a hospital, sick with the measles. There are nurses and doctors here to take good care of you." Hilda sighed, moved her head more comfortably on the pillow and visibly relaxed.

Ok, one girl more comfortable, Abigail thought and flew to Kate's bed. Kate was still sitting bolt upright in her bed, staring at the ceiling and blinking back tears. This time Abigail did not hesitate. She sat on Kate's shoulder and began to sing:

Over in Killarney, many years ago
Me Mither sang a song to me in tones so sweet and low,
Just a simple little ditty, in her good old Irish way,
And I'd give the world if she could sing That song to me this day.

Too-ra-loo-ra-loo-ral,
Too-ra-loo-ra-li,
Too-ra-loo-ra-loo-ral,
Hush now don't you cry!
Too-ra-loo-ra-loo-ral,
Too-ra-loo-ra-li,
Too-ra-loo-ra-loo-ral,
That's an Irish lullaby.

Bennett began laughing. "This one I recognize right away! My Grandpa used to sing this to me all the time." Abigail sang the second verse:

Oft, in dreams I wander
To that cot again,
I feel her arms a huggin' me
As when she held me then.
And I hear her voice a hummin'
To me as in days of yore,
When she used to rock me fast asleep
Outside the cabin door.

Kate put her head on the pillow, but the tears flowed down her cheeks.

Abigail whispered, "Do not worry. You are sick but you will get better. You are in good hands. The hospital staff will take good care of you."

But Kate still sighed.

"Where's me mother?" Kate mumbled. "Why did she abandon me here?"

"She did not abandon you," whispered Abigail. "The immigration health rules require her to stay with your siblings so they will not catch your sickness."

Abigail sang the "Too-ra-loo-ra" chorus again and slowly Kate closed her eyes.

Abigail flew back up to the rafters to the Fairy Group. "What should I tell them about their parents?" fretted Abigail.

"Nothing for now. First we have to find out what happens to them, so we know what to say!" said Enjella.

CHAPTER NINE

Reunited

"Bennett, remember how we started this adventure?"

"With Tom McGlew's note pinned to MY pajamas!"

"Right!" said Alicia, beginning the motion to wave her wand.

Enjella arrested the wand in mid-swoop, with a quick zap. "Save the fanfare, Alicia. It IS getting old."

"Never gets old," muttered Alicia, but she dropped her arm.

"What building is Tom in now?" asked Bennett.

"That boy can't still be here!" exclaimed Abigail. "We met him six years ago."

Bennett scratched his head. "Oh, right. We saw him when we first arrived here, and that was in 1908. This time twisting gets confusing."

"But we did not get to see him leave."

"Whoa, wait!" said Alicia, "of course we did. Remember the Kissing Post, and the man with the..."

"The KISSING Post! We definitely did NOT..." said Abigail.

"Whoa. My mistake," said Alicia. The rest of Abigail's sentence was lost in space, or maybe time, as the Fairies twisted time again and brought them back to 1908.

"Gee, these cages really do look scary! It was much nicer up here without them. The Registry Room in the Grand Hall is certainly not a warm fuzzy place," said Abigail.

"It is WAY more crowded than in 1914. How the heck does anyone even hear himself think? So many people talking all at once," declared Bennett.

"You, at least, are hearing it all in your own language, so it makes sense. Imagine what everyone down there hears," said Enjella.

"Babble, babble, babble," said Alicia.

"That's not very nice!" said Enjella, hands on her hips. Pop! Fireworks shot from her head.

"OH, no! No! No!" said Alicia, "I did not mean YOU. I meant..." she slapped her knee, "that was a good one! I am funnier than I think I am.

"I meant, all the voices from all the people in many languages just blend together to create a big hubbub, which just sounds like babble."

"Apology accepted," snapped Enjella.

"I did not apologize," began Alicia.

"Ahem," said Abigail. "I believe someone mentioned the Kissing Post."

"Look!" said Bennett. The group followed the direction of his finger and looked straight down. There was the boy, with the note still pinned to his rumpled jacket. He was looking anxiously through the cages at a small room on the other side of the large waiting room, where a door kept opening to admit people from the outside. Almost every time the door opened, a single man came in; there were very few women, and very few groups of people who entered. The official standing inside the door stopped each arrival, asked for his name and the names of the people the man was here to meet. Scrutinizing entries on the sheets of papers in front of him, he located the immigrants' name. The official then verified that everything was in order. If satisfied, he called out a family name.

Each time, family members on the Time Travelers' and boy's side of the cage would either shout with joy or silently scurry to the opening where the official would check their papers against his book, and then open the gate for them to meet their loved one.

If no one answered the summons, the official would dispatch someone to the other waiting areas, the dormitories, and the dining rooms, to find the lucky relatives of the person waiting to take them to their new homes.

One joyful reunion was happier than the next. A mother carrying a baby, with two little girls clinging to her skirts, ran out the door. The mother and baby jumped right into the man's arms, the mother crying with joy.

The man's eyes filled with tears as he held them both in a tight embrace. He gently put the mother down, lifted her chin and gave her a kiss. She blushed and giggled. The man hugged each little girl in turn. They grabbed his legs and hung on. "Papa! Papa!" they shouted.

The man turned his attention to the baby in his wife's arms.

"This is your newest daughter," said the woman, handing the man a six-month-old baby.

"Until today I have only read about you! My joy is complete. I see my children all safe in America." The family walked out in one big knot, still hugging, with bags and parcels hanging on their elbows and balancing on their heads.

The History Explorers grinned at each other, feeling the happiness of the reunited family.

Meanwhile Tom sat on the bench looking glum, humming "Too-ra-loo-ra-loo-ral."

As they all watched, yet another single man walked through the outside door and checked in with the officials.

"And what do you have in that big bundle?" questioned the Ellis Island staff member.

"American clothes for my family!" said the man.

The official gave a grin and turned to find his family.

A woman with two boys and two girls, in rumpled, threadbare clothes, came running and hugged the man. Everyone talked at once in Hungarian.

"Ok, we have a long ferry ride to keep talking," said the father holding up his hand. "Now you change, then we go!"

"Change?" said the woman. Even though they spoke in Hungarian, the Time Travelers heard everything in English.

"Yes, I bring for you American clothes," said the man in English, and puffed out his chest with pride.

"What? Why? What are you talking about?" said the mother. The children clamored around to see what was in the bundle, and began to pull out pants for the boys and a dress for each of the girls.

The man explained in Hungarian, "I do not want my family to look like poor beggars from the old country. Take off those patched, worn clothes that are dirty from travel. Today we start a new life as an American family. We are no longer peasants, we are hardworking Americans and we will look like Americans!"

The children were very excited and began changing clothes right then and there. The mother did not want to change at all. But the father insisted.

"Look! Look at the pretty, modern clothes!" he said, trying to talk her into it. He held out a beautiful jacket and tried to put it on the woman over her old one. It did not fit. The woman looked uncertain, but she finally took off her old jacket and put on the new one. Now it fit her perfectly and looked beautiful. Encouraged, the woman reached into the bundle and took out another piece of clothing.

"I do not even know what part of the body this is for!" exclaimed the woman, holding up an article that had a hole as if for a head, feathers and beads, but no openings for arms. She held it one way, she held it another, but she could not figure it out. She wrapped it around her like a shawl, but the hole gapped and hung down. She pulled it off and threw it to the man.

"It is for neck," he said, and put it around his neck. The officials laughed.

"Maybe for arm?" he said, putting one big arm through the hole. The feathers flew and the material draped down to the floor. Now everyone in both rooms was watching, and people were smiling and laughing.

The man brought it over to one of the officials. "Please help! What for a piece of clothing?" he asked.

The official picked it up and held it this way and that. "Well it sure beats me!" he finally exclaimed. "Maybe if I had a wife or a sister I would know what to do with that darn thing!"

"Papa, these pants are too short!" interrupted the oldest boy.

One of the girls laughed and pointed to her little brother. "And Stanislaw's pants are too big! You must switch!"

The children finished dressing and each proudly circled their father, wearing their American clothes. The mother just stood there, shaking her head, looking at the silly garment, twisting it this way and that.

"Come, come," said the man, turning back to his wife, "we wrap it on your head like so!" and he wrapped it turban style around her head, with the feathers grandly sticking out on top.

Everyone laughed and clapped.

"Let us go to meet America!" he announced and the group left amid the applause. The History Explorers laughed and somersaulted in the air until they looked down at Tom.

Amid all of the laughter, the Irish boy still waited anxiously, jumping up every time the door would open, only to flop down in disappointment when strangers emerged.

Bennett looked down at the boy's head. "When is it going to be his turn?" he asked the Fairies. They just shrugged their shoulders.

"You have to wait and see," chortled Alicia. "Waiting intensifies the drama!"

Bennett looked at Enjella for help. Enjella would not answer directly either, "One of the hardest parts for most of the immigrants was the WAITING."

Tom started shaking his head and muttering. The Time Travelers zoomed a bit closer so they could hear:

"It's getting on toward the end of the day. I can't bear another night. I canna sleep in the woman's dormitory without Aunt Eileen. There's no place fer me in the men's dorm, and I won't sleep in that big baggage room with no decent place to lay me head again!"

Bennett's heart reached out to the boy. "Can you make me visible, dressed in the clothing of the day? Maybe I can go talk to him?" he finally asked.

The two Fairies looked at each other. In an instant they were just a swirl of sparkles as they conferred with each other.

"THOMAS CHARLES MCGLEW!" shouted the official.

The boy looked up, dazed, and looked around at the people in the room. "Well that's me, but where's me dad?"

The two Fairies stopped sparkling and spinning.

A tall, broad shouldered, well-fed man stood smiling into the cages. When he saw Tom looking around he took his cap off his head and beamed even more broadly.

The official pointed him out to the boy.

Tom shook his head 'no'. "Me dad's a skinny chap, bent over from hard work and no food, and he's got a fine beard by blarney. Someone here is mistaken."

"Son-o-mine!" shouted his Dad, "I'm in America now! Here we stand proud and tall. I have been well fed. I do an honest day of labor and everyone in the household can eat well!"

"Pa! It do sound like you, but where's your beard!" Tom, cap in hand, small bag at his feet, looked hopeful.

"Shaved off so's I can look presentable for me important job."

The boy still looked unsure.

"I am the foreman of the maintenance crew of The New Croton Aqueduct," the father said proudly. Tommy just looked at him blankly. "'Tis a grand enterprise. Provid'n water to the entire City o' New York."

Tom still stood staring at the man, unsure.

"This whole process would have been a mite easier if'n I just coulda come two days ago, when yer Uncle Mike picked up yer Aunt Eileen. She would have recognized me! I surely hope they made it to Philadelphia aright.

"Come, son! 'Tis your own flesh an' blood, what rocked ye in yer granddad's old rocker with the carving of a hen on the top!"

"The hen rocker! OH PA!" Tom ran into the man's arms and hugged him hard. Mr. McGlew's muscular arms wrapped so completely around the small boy that Tommy disappeared in the bear hug.

Alicia wiped a tear from her eyes. "Group hug!" she said. And the History Explorers were only too happy to fly in for a big hug. Pop! Sparkles and stars swirled around their heads and children floated effortlessly with happiness, their wings not even flapping.

Alicia pulled away finally and did one more 'happy dance'.

Bennett followed her lead and danced with her.

"That was beautiful," sighed Abigail.

"Yes," said Enjella. "There were many heartwarming endings to the long, arduous immigration journey. So many happy family reunions took place right in this room. It makes you glad to be alive! Such wonderful, love-filled, joyous moments."

"Yes, wonderful," agreed Bennett. "But why did we come all the way back here to see his reunion with his Dad? Why is it so important?"

"Is it not rewarding enough for you Bennett, just to see their happiness?" teased Alicia.

"Well of course," stammered Bennett. "But…"

"Enchanted Elbows, I am only teasing," said Alicia. "We needed you to observe several things about Tommy and his reunion with his father."

Wisps of mysterious fog encircled Enjella's head and she said, "Tommy McGlew is a critical player in the part of the drama yet to unfold."

CHAPTER TEN

Strange Spaghetti

Before they could even blink, the children found themselves back in the Measles Ward.

"WHEN are we now?" asked Bennett.

"Exactly when we left off to go to the Kissing Room," informed Alicia.

Bennett observed, "Those poor sick girls did not move since we left!"

"Because we have only been gone a blink-of-an-eye," said Alicia.

"Is that some kind of an official amount of time?" asked Bennett.

"It is in Sparkleshire," said Enjella, crossing her arms over her chest.

"Ok, Ok," said Bennett. "We just do not use that time measurement on earth that often any more."

"Resuming our mission then," said Enjella, "Abigail was just successful as an invisible voice calming the girls' fears."

"We can SEE that," said Bennett. The Time Travelers looked down on the slumbering girls.

ZAAP! Alicia's wand flashed out and back so quickly Abigail was unsure whether or not she had really seen it.

"It is now four days later," announced Alicia.

"Wait," said Bennett, "why couldn't we have just come to NOW in the first place, instead of going back to a 'blink-of-an-eye' later than when we left?"

"Then you would not have learned about that Fairy unit of time!" smiled Alicia.

Bennett shook his head, "Icky Ishkabibble!"

Enjella cleared her throat. "Ahem! But we digress! Back to our task at hand: to help these girls through a very difficult time. Since they were fast asleep "in a blink of an eye," I thought we should wait until their fevers subsided a bit before getting started. Now they have had four days of rest and are beginning to recuperate. They are just beginning to feel a little bit more like themselves. The nurses and hospital staff have given them wonderful care, but nobody has explained anything to them; in fact I don't think anyone has even talked to them yet."

"Why haven't the girls asked the nurses what was happening?" Bennett wanted to know. "Why don't they speak up for themselves?"

"It was a time when children were trained to be seen but not heard," said Enjella.

"Is it too much bother to tell the patients what is going on?" demanded Abigail, her hand on her hips. "Don't the nurses care?"

Enjella and Alicia both said, "Of course they do!"

"But there are so many patients and there is just too much work to do. The nurses must treat the patients' symptoms: take temperatures, reduce fevers, give cooling sponge baths, dispense medicine, water, and food, try to make patients more comfortable. And at the same time they must keep records and track the illness of each patient on their medical charts. They are so busy there is little time to even think about other things," said Enjella.

Alicia pointed to some women walking through the aisles of beds, "Volunteers have come to bring books and little gifts for the children. They try to talk to the patients, but often there is a language barrier. Our two girls, unfortunately, were always sleeping during the volunteer visits. Patients need to sleep – the volunteers are not allowed to wake them. Reading to patients and even talking to them was thought to be frivolous, or at best, optional," said Enjella.

"At least a volunteer left each girl a book," observed Abigail, pointing to the foot of the bed, where a picture book lay.

"That must be from the Ellis Island library," said Bennett. "I wonder if the girls know the books are there?"

"Thank heavens for the volunteers!" shouted Alicia executing a cartwheel. Pop! "Hip Hip Hooray!" she shouted, waving pompoms and continuing her cartwheels. Then she grew serious. "It was quite a difficult job for the 357 employees of Ellis Island to process the tens of thousands of people who entered the United States here. But it was an even more difficult job to care for the sick immigrants."

Alicia turned. Pop! A chart with a big red line zigzagging across a grid appeared on an easel. Alicia pointed with a pointer. "In 1907, Ellis Island had its busiest day ever: Eleven THOUSAND people were screened in ONE day! That night, there were thousands of people detained here, sleeping in the waiting areas, the dormitories and of course the hospitals."

"With numbers like that…"

"And no computers to help," interjected Bennett.

Alicia nodded. "…you can see why it may have been hard for employees to not lose their patience, much less than try to think of reassuring things to say to the immigrants.

"Furthermore, people during that time were generally too busy trying to survive and feed themselves to think about feelings!" said Alicia, throwing her head back and putting her hand to her temple in a melodramatic pose. Pop! A song blared from an old fashioned record player: 'FEELINGS, oh whoa whoa Feelings.' Alicia pulled a handkerchief out of thin air and began to weep loudly. Tears spurted everywhere, spraying Bennett and Abigail. Alicia wrung her handkerchief into a bucket. Water splashed everywhere and then overflowed the bucket.

Suddenly it all evaporated.

"That was quite the dramatic moment, Alicia," Enjella said. She put her hand up over her mouth, but not before they saw the grin she was trying to cover.

She cleared her throat. "We must explain the situation to the girls:

they are sick, but are in a new hospital and well provided for…"

"Can you dress me in an assistant nurse's uniform?" asked Abigail. "Then even if someone sees me, I can explain what is happening and it will not look suspicious."

Before Abigail even finished her sentence, both Fairies pulled out their wands and zapped her. A sparkle floated down over her, changing her clothes into a pink and white starched dress, apron and little nurse's hat.

"You are a candy-striper!" exclaimed Alicia, clapping her hands and wearing a similar pink-and-white-striped outfit.

"What the heck is that?" asked Bennett.

"It is a girl hospital volunteer," said Alicia.

"I don't know that they would have had candy-stripers in Ellis Island," frowned Enjella. "In fact I don't think they invented them until the 1950s."

Alicia stamped her foot and waved her wand. "By the time we make sure everyone approves of Abigail's clothes, it will be too late to send her down."

Enjella raised her eyebrows, but merely said, "Ready?" to Abigail who nodded. She then magically appeared in between the girls' beds, human size and visible again.

The trio remaining saw her lean down to whisper, first to Kate and then to Hilda. Both girls stared straight ahead; they did not even look at her.

At last they both sighed and closed their eyes. Enjella zapped Abigail back up into the rafters.

"Now we are just going to watch them sleep?" asked Bennett with a frown.

"Patience. Patience," said Enjella.

A few minutes passed. Nothing happened. The two girls just lay there with their eyes closed. The silence echoed loudly in the large room. The rest of the children on the other side of the ward either slept or stared around glumly.

Suddenly Bennett said, "MMMMM! What do I smell?"

"Spaghetti and meatballs," said Alicia. Pop! A plate of steaming spaghetti topped by two plump meatballs sat on top of her head. Spaghetti ran down the sides of the plate and laced itself in her hair. More spaghetti slid down her nose and hung off her ears.

"Interesting look," said Abigail.

"But even better smell," said Bennett. "I am hungry!"

Plates of spaghetti appeared in their hands as a cart stacked with dishes of spaghetti dinners appeared at the large room's entrance. Hospital kitchen staff wheeled the cart through the ward, bringing plates of the warm meal to each patient.

Twirling their spaghetti and slurping happily on their own heaping plates, the History Explorers watched the two girls sit up in bed, interested in the good smell, in spite of their illness. But instead of looking happy when they got the plates, they just looked puzzled.

A shy look passed between the girls, as they both warily looked at the plates of spaghetti.

"'Tis a small bit o' fortune, I am not hungry," said Kate turning toward Hilda, "for I could not for the life o' me think what this could be. Do you know?" She timidly thrust her fork into the spaghetti. She moved it back and forth. As she lifted her fork some of the spaghetti strands came with it, but then they unstuck, sliding off the fork, down the side of the plate and on to the tray.

"Ja," Hilda gave a ghost of a smile, but she shook her head no. She winced, put down her folk and turned her head away.

"Wait," said Bennett, with his mouth full of the delicious pasta, "she said 'yes' but she shook her head 'no'. Which one does she mean?"

"Haven't they ever seen spaghetti before?" asked Abigail, so surprised that she forgot to swallow.

"Spaghetti would not be served in either of their homelands," advised Enjella looking scholarly.

"If you think that is funny," said Alicia, "wait until you see what they do with the banana!"

As if on cue, Hilda picked up the banana on her tray, sniffed it, and then put it down. Kate glanced over at her, picked up her own banana and tried to take a bite out of it, through the skin.

"Can I fly down to her and tell her what to do?" asked Bennett.

"I don't think they are going to have much faith in a mysterious voice in their ears giving them eating instructions," said Abigail.

"That is right!' said Bennett "we need to be visible, dressed in the right clothes. Then we can actually help when we visit them."

"And we can't be Fairy size," agreed Abigail.

"In good time," said Enjella. "Right now they are both too sick to eat much." The crew looked down and saw that each girl had nibbled about half of her meatball. Then they put down their forks.

The two Fairies touched the children's elbows.

"Why did it just get darker?" said Bennett.

"We have advanced time ten days," advised Enjella.

"Can't you just once tell us the plan ahead of time?" complained Bennett.

"Where would the fun be in that?" said Alicia. She tapped him on the elbow and they disappeared!

"Where did they go?" said Abigail.

"They are on a mission!"

"Don't we get to go too?" asked Abigail, looking disappointed.

"We have our work cut out for us here," said Enjella. "Look below. Neither girl is contagious now. In 1914 the nurses would not yet be sure of that fact, so both girls will still be quarantined for a little while longer. But they are both beginning to feel much better. They still have had little conversation with anyone here. And even though they have exchanged glances with each other, they have not spoken to each other since their exchange over the spaghetti dinner.

"So what are we going to do about that?" said Abigail.

"I am afraid I cannot do anything. It is up to you Kiddo," replied Enjella.

"Put me in clothes an American girl would wear in New York in 1914, and I will go down and talk to them," said Abigail.

"Maybe you should re-think that!" said Enjella. Abigail looked confused. "The stylish clothes of an American girl in New York City might be noticed among the immigrant girls."

"Oh, I get it." Abigail forced a smile. She was sorry that she would not get to wear fine fashionable clothing, but she knew she was there for a more important reason than to just try out the 1900s styles. "Give me immigrant clothing," she said with conviction. She leaned over to Enjella and whispered, "But could you make it something colorful?"

Enjella smiled and zapped her wand. "The clothes from Tuscany, Italy were nice and bright. Many immigrants came from Italy at this time."

"I'll blend!" said Abigail.

With another zap of the wand Abigail was standing in between the beds of the two girls. "Wait!" she said. "Won't the nurses catch me?"

"Not at this time. They are busy doing rounds and dispensing medicine. They figure the children in this ward will be okay while they eat."

"OK. Make me visible."

"Ah!" Both girls saw Abigail at the same time and stared curiously at her.

Abigail looked down at her clothes to make sure the seams of her stockings were straight. *Boy is this clothing uncomfortable! The cotton material in this dress is so heavy and so shapeless. I certainly am glad that stretchy fabric blends were invented,* Abigail thought.

Suddenly she realized she was a little nervous. She licked her lips, "Good evening." Through Fairy magic Hilda heard her in German, while Kate heard her in English, but with a slight Irish brogue, so she sounded familiar.

Both girls' faces lit up. They each turned to her but did not say anything.

Now what? Abigail thought. Instinctively, she started singing again.

This time the Irish folk song "When Irish Eyes Are Smiling" sprang to her lips.

Kate smiled a huge smile and joined in. Hilda watched them closely with a small smile on her face, not joining in, for she did not know the words of course, but every now and then she would hum along with the melody.

All three girls laughed shyly when the song was over.

"I am sure you already figured this out," Abigail's words were again magically translated so each girl heard her in her own language. "This is a hospital. You had the measles, and now, thanks to the doctors and nurses here, you are almost completely recovered."

"Yes, Nurse Colligan is surely a wee bit o' Ireland come here to help me," said Kate. "She held my hand while she took my temperature, and smiled an angel's smile at me."

"Everyone here is very good at their job," said Hilda, in German, to Abigail. "They are very efficient."

Abigail sat down on Kate's bed. She reached for her hand and formally introduced Kate to Hilda. The girls smiled at each other, still a little shy, but encouraged after speaking to Abigail.

Enjella whispered in Abigail's ear, "Keep telling Hilda the English word for simple things, so she can accumulate a vocabulary."

"But how can I do that, when I all I am speaking is English?" asked Abigail.

"Magic!" smiled Enjella. "The magic will know when you say 'the English word is…' or even 'the word is…'"

"Tricky," said Abigail. She turned back to Hilda and asked her if she liked spaghetti now.

"Yes," said Hilda in English, but she shook her head no.

Kate and Abigail giggled. "Yes?" asked Kate, shaking her head yes.

"Or 'No'," said Abigail, shaking her head 'no'."

"No," said Hilda, shaking her head 'yes'.

Enjella flew to Abigail's ear. "Explain to her 'Yes' and 'No' again."

"Do you mean, *ja*, or in English 'Yes'," said Abigail in German, shaking her head 'yes', "you do like spaghetti, or *nein*, 'NO'," Abigail shook her head 'no', "you do not like spaghetti."

"Ahhh," said Hilda, "Yes, is ja," she shook her head 'yes'. "I was very confused!"

The three young girls all giggled again.

"Do you know where my mother is?" both girls asked at almost the same time.

Abigail frowned. "I don't exactly…"

The smile on both girls' faces immediately disappeared. They stared down at their blankets, tears welling in their eyes.

"Why did my mother just leave me here, alone?" said Kate.

"Why have I been abandoned in this strange new country?" asked Hilda.

"Your mothers did not want to leave you here. The health rules required that you be taken into the Contagious Disease Ward and be quarantined. Both of your mothers wanted to come with you, but they were not allowed. I do not know SPECIFICALLY where they are, but I am pretty sure your families are fine."

"I believe Hilda, your mother and sister were met by your father. Your family is working hard to establish a business in New York City, while they anxiously wait for you to get better." Hilda looked a little happier to hear that, but still the corners of her mouth were turned down.

"Ja," she said, but she sadly shook her head "no".

Abigail turned to Kate, "I am not sure where your mother is, but I will find out!" She said 'good night' to them and walked out of the big ward room to the corridor.

"Where is Kate's mother?" she asked Enjella.

"In another ward of this hospital!" said Enjella.

CHAPTER ELEVEN

Hot Potato

Bennett took a deep breath. "Ok, I get that you like to surprise me. But couldn't you at least give me a hint about what we are going to do? I see we are at the Kissing Post again. Did we change time?"

"Bennett, your mission, IF you decide to accept it," intoned Alicia with a dramatic sweep of a cape which suddenly draped down her back, "will be undercover, and a bit more complicated than you may be expecting!"

"Okay," said Bennett, "now we are getting somewhere!"

"Yeah, the Meeting Room," joked Alicia.

"Almost on our way to freedom," said Bennett. "Are the girls ready to be released? Are they going to be reunited with their families?"

"Not so fast, nor so easy, I am afraid," said Alicia. Pop! Her hair was silver with worry. Many silver pendants and huge dangling many-tiered earrings appeared on her head. The jewelry shook and shivered, as if in fear. "Do you recognize anyone in this room?"

Bennett took his time to scrutinize the people, mostly men, waiting on the 'free' side of the Kissing Post. No one looked the least bit familiar. For a few minutes the boy and Fairy hovered overhead as names were called, and families just finished being processed were united with relatives who had already successfully immigrated.

"It's a quarter of an hour before seven. Almost quitting time," shouted an inspector, when there were only two men left in the room. One, a big burly gentleman from Latvia, stepped forward and the inspector bellowed his family's name. A woman with two children rushed forward. The cage door was opened. Amid hugs and kisses and tears, the family soon departed for the ferry to New Jersey.

"Well it is obvious now," said Alicia. "There is only one boy left!"

One young man sat on a bench, whistling, "It's a Long Long Way to Tipperary."

"Boy?" asked Bennett, "You mean that tall muscular guy, whistling, with the hat pulled low? He is no boy."

Alicia pulled out all her hair, and turned to Bennett. "That's Tommy McGlew!" she said. Pop! Her hair magically attached itself back to her head. "Doing the math," Pop! A chalkboard appeared with 1914 minus 1908 written on it, "he is now sixteen years old."

"Itchy Ishkabibble!" said Bennett, "being an American really agrees with him!"

"Indubitably!" said Alicia. "He wasn't kidding when he said all he had eaten in Ireland in the year before he came to the U.S. was potato gruel. Now he is properly nourished and a strong lad."

"So now what?"

"It is almost time for the inspectors to close for the night and go home. Tom is looking for his family. He and his father read in the newspaper that the ship, the SS CEDRIC, carrying more of their family members arrived. But his father had to leave on business overseas. In fact, Mr. Charles McGlew's ship probably sailed right by the CEDRIC docked in the New York Harbor. So Tommy is here to meet them. However, there is a problem; Tommy can't find them. That is where you come in."

"But I don't even know who his family is!"

"Don't you though?" teased Alicia. "A HINT: his sister is in quarantine."

Bennett still looked puzzled. "There are dozens of kids in quarantine! All those kids in the with the infectious head disease in the Favus Ward, all the kids with mumps and the all the kids with Kate and Hilda in the Measles Ward..."

"Yes..." Alicia shook her head encouragingly.

Bennett started pulling his own hair.

"When Irish Eyes Are Smiling," Bennett looked down to hear Tom singing softly to himself.

"Hey, I know that song. My Grandpa sang it to me all the time."

"ME eyes won't be smiling much longer if I can't find me Mother," muttered Tom.

Alicia flew right in front of Bennett's eyes. "Focus!" she said, her two fingers pointing at Bennett's eyes, and then at her own. "You are thinking too globally! HINT number TWO – we watched the first time she ate spaghetti."

"Hilda?"

"Does Hilda look like Tommy McGlew? Why do I have to spell everything out for you?" Pop! An enormous dictionary appeared on Alicia's head, with K-A-T-E spelled in large letters on the top of the open page.

"Just kidding. I knew it was Kate," grinned Bennett, starting to whistle 'When Irish Eyes Are Smiling' along with Tom.

ZAAAAP!

Bennett found himself outside on the lawn of the main administrative building. The door burst open and Tommy McGlew stumbled out.

"They don't know who she is! They don't know where they are! How can that be? Someone must know something!" Tommy mumbled to himself, punching the air in frustration.

Bennett nervously stepped forward, full sized, visible, and dressed in period clothes, hoping for the magic words to calm Tom.

Alicia waved her magic wand in the soft dusk of the June evening. To a casual observer, she looked like a firefly.

Bennett opened his mouth to speak, and his words came out in a lilting Irish brogue. "I know something o' yer sister!"

Tommy McGlew looked startled, but came closer to hear.

"Whadda ya know?" he said.

"She contracted the measles on the crossing. She is being cared for at the hospital in quarantine."

Tommy looked alarmed. He staggered backward a bit. "Oh the poor wee tyke! Sick and in Hospital! Saint Brigid preserve her! And me poor mother, sitting by the bed fretting! Thinkin' o the many in our village who lost children to this disease."

"Do not fret, she is getting excellent care," said Bennett. "But your mother is not with her. They don't allow the families to enter the quarantine unit."

"Saints preserve us, no! Me family canna afford excellent care. This will cause hardship for father. Sure, now he's been promoted to shipping engineer. But he spent some of his savings sailing back over to Ireland last October to check on the family. And the rest of all he had saved, could beg or borrow went to pay passage for the rest o' the family."

Tommy, saddled with apprehension, tugged at one red curl dangling over his forehead. He started pacing back and forth. Suddenly, another worry struck him. "Whadda ya mean, me mother's not with her? Where's me mother?" he stopped short with alarm.

"Get a hold of yourself now," said Bennett. "Your sister is recuperating well, and I can take you to see her. But first we must locate your mother, so we can tell her that you are here, and that your sister is almost well enough to be released."

"Well I don't know who ye are, little fellow, but the man in there is too busy to give me answers. So I am going to have to trust ye to he'p me. What is the plan?'

"What is the plan?" repeated Bennett. Alicia buzzed around his head, invisible to Tommy.

"No I'm ask'n ye what is the plan?" asked Tommy.

"No really, what is the plan?" Bennett reached out and grabbed Alicia by the wing.

"Are ye a mischievous little leprechaun, come to vex me more than help me?" said Tommy, a flush creeping up his face to the roots of his red hair.

"I'm sure there IS a plan," muttered Bennett through clenched teeth, looking at Alicia.

Zap! Alicia froze Tommy – and Bennett sighed with relief. "Now you really HAVE to tell me the plan, or we have just made poor Tom's life more miserable, instead of helping him."

"Ok, get in a huddle!"

"Just the two of us?" Bennett rolled his eyes. "Can't we just get to the plan part?"

"OK," said Alicia, stamping her foot. "Gosh, way to take the fun out of it!

"I know where the service entrance to the kitchen is. We can get into the dining room through the delivery area. Once inside, you and Tommy can blend with the rest of the immigrants and find his mother, brother and other sister. They will be so excited to see Tommy, they won't even ask about Kate. But then, while you eat you can tell them they should be able to leave within the next few days. Imagine their happiness when you tell them Kate is almost fully recuperated, and Tommy is there to prove they have family that will take care of them and support them in America. Foolproof, right?

"Any questions?"

Bennett thought very hard. He hesitated, scratching his head. "I can't think of any questions, exactly. But I can think of a million things that could go wrong, all leading us to getting caught, and detained, and maybe even causing the family to be deported!"

"There are always a million things that could go wrong!" twinkled Alicia. "That's what makes this such an exciting adventure!"

"You are SO bad at cheering me up," said Bennett with a frown.

Alicia slapped him on the back, "Buck up, me boy. Don't forget, we have one thing they don't."

"What is that?" asked Bennett.

"Magic!" said Alicia. "Our most important asset. How could you forget about that?"

"YOU'VE got the magic. I only have it when you feel like sharing it with me," said Bennett.

"That's way better than any other human here, don't forget." Alicia waved her wand and time unfroze.

"Come this way," said Bennett with a wave of his arm.

"Lucky leprechaun, lead the way to me family!" said Tommy.

Following the invisible Alicia, Bennett led Tom McGlew around the back of the main administrative building. Sticking close to the building shadows cast by the evening sun, Bennett thought, *Shoot! I forgot we twisted time to June! It is almost the longest day of the year. If it were winter, we would have the cover of darkness at dinnertime. Now we have to be EXTRA careful sneaking around.*

His heart beat rapidly as he tried to visualize how this plan would work.

CRASH! Rattle rattle rattle KER- plop!

Bennett was thinking so hard, watching the shadows and looking for staff workers or security guards who might catch them, that he stepped on a metal lid, blown off a garbage can by the wind from the ocean.

Two men who had been lounging against the side of the building smoking cigarettes called out, "Who goes there?"

Bennett and Tom looked at each other in distress. The men stared harder.

"I see you boys," said one of the men harshly.

Bennett's heart pounded. Alicia raised her wand and pointed it toward Bennett. *Ishkabibble!* he thought, *if we run away, Alicia can make me invisible, but what would happen to Tom?* Hesitating, Bennett thought frantically, trying to come up with a strategy.

In a low voice, Tom asked, " Is this part o' the plan, little leprechaun?"

"UHHHH. . . ?" said Bennett.

The two men started to walk toward them, their chef's hats bouncing up and down on their heads. "Where are your uniforms?" shouted one of them.

Thinking even faster, Bennett said, "Ye caught us red-handed. We've not yet put on our uniforms. Many apologies, Sirs. We were heading to the kitchen right now to find our aprons."

"Ye did the set up of the tables without yer white coats?" growled the taller man. "I'll be talking to the boss and recommending a docking of pay."

"I understand Sir," said Bennett, looking appropriately contrite. "That would only be right. But we'll rectify that directly." He grabbed Tom's arm and pulled him into the nearest open doorway.

"But the uniforms are by the supply closet," shouted the shorter man. "What's a matter with yer brains tonight lad?"

Bennett popped his head back out, "So right, Sir. But I do not want to further irritate you by parading in front of you without the proper attire. You can be sure, the next time you see us we will be properly dressed."

Tom turned to him, scratching his head. "We will?"

Bennett whispered, as he pulled him along a corridor. "Here's the plan: we don some uniforms, and then we help serve the dinner. That way we will be able to see all of the detained immigrants at all three dinner sittings."

Tom looked a bit confused.

"Remember," Bennett said, "there are hundreds and hundreds of people detained here tonight, and it will take three sittings to feed all of them. We might be detected if we just show up and try to eat dinner. But even if no one catches us, how could we make sure we can find your family? What if we picked the wrong dinner sitting and your family was not there?"

Tom broke out in a huge grin. "Quite the clever leprechaun, aren't we?" They strolled along the corridor. Tom started whistling, "It's a Long Long Way to Tipperary" again.

Bennett started singing it.

"Now how do ye know that tune?" asked Tom.

"My grandfather used to sing it to me," said Bennett.

"Now I know you are one of the enchanted folk for certain!" exclaimed Tom. "That song was just written! 'Tis not even widely known yet! I only know it because me Father came back from Ireland humming it two months ago."

Bennett was at a loss for words. *OOOOPS!* he thought.

Alicia twinkled up and down in front of Bennett's nose. He did not react. Pop! A big neon sign appeared and she pointed behind him with it. He still was searching for something to say to Tom. Alicia spun Bennett around to face where she was pointing. Bennett finally noticed a large sign on a door in the corridor: KITCHEN PANTRY.

"Jackpot," he said, opening the door and pulling Tom inside. The large storage room contained tall wooden shelves with boxes and bins of onions and other root vegetables, fresh herbs, stacks of cans, hundreds of dishes, and rows and rows of miscellaneous supplies. A rolling laundry cart of clean white waiter's jackets was parked in front of one of the big canisters of milk.

What luck! thought Bennett, pulling two jackets out of the fresh laundry pile.

"By all the Saints in Ireland," said Tom. "Have ye ever, in all yer born days, seen so many luscious potatoes?" He walked over to the overflowing potato bin. "So plump, so compelling," he picked one up. "They seem to be calling my name." He put his ear to the potato. In a high pitched voice he said, "Tom, feast yer eyes on me and me brother lumpers. Think o' all the mashed potatoes yer'd be making out o' us spuds. White and creamy; dripping with butter…"

Alicia merrily did cartwheels over his head.

"Get a hold of yourself, Tom," said Bennett, "TOM!"

"Aye, yer right," said Tom, putting down the potato and blushing. "Me imagination gets pretty carried away. But I had many a hungry night back in the old country dreaming o' the lumper, since I saw a precious few in the skin." He patted his stomach. "And I haven't had a proper meal since I set out here to Ellis Island to find me kin."

Alicia's hair went limp and her wings deflated. She started drifting down toward the ground.

"But yer all right now, eh Tom?" asked Bennett with a worried look on his face.

"Yessur!" reassured Tom. Alicia zoomed up and sat on a potato. "Ever since I stepped foot in America, I have been eating me fill. I know I can be assured of a fine meal once I am back in Croton-on-Hudson. T'was unheard of before I got to America. A bit o'me is always worried that I'll wake up and be back to me skinny, starvin' self."

Bennett breathed a sigh with deep feeling for the poor hungry boy. "Well, hopefully we can find a bite to eat here. But we must stay focused so that yer siblings can enjoy these fine victuals."

Bennett looked at Alicia, still twinkling on top of a potato, now uncharacteristically quiet. She jumped up and suddenly, silently, executed a few cartwheels that sent off streamers. Bennett scratched his head, trying to figure out what she was up to, when the streamers re-arranged themselves into a sign: NICE WORK BENNETT! He smiled. Then he squinted. Another sign appeared, in smaller print: GOOD JOB BLENDING BY USING OLD FASHIONED LANGUAGE.

"I didn't know you knew those words," Alicia said and did one final cartwheel. Bennett shook his head, but with a grin.

Quickly the boys donned the jackets and walked back out of the building toward the dining hall. The two chefs walked toward them again, and Bennett's heart leapt into his throat. Alicia zipped ahead. Bennett quickened his pace to get away from them and Tom trotted along behind him, but it was no use; the men caught up with them.

One reached out his hand and clapped Bennett on the back.

Oh no! thought Bennett breaking out in a sweat.

But the man grinned, "That's better now. All suited up proper. We must take our jobs seriously, there's good lads. Now look lively, the first crowd is soon to be upon us. A cool head and quick feet will serve you well to serve them well."

Bennett let his breath out in a big puff of air. He hadn't realized he was so apprehensive that he had been holding it in. He said, "You don't know how true that is Sir."

The boys, accompanied by the men, walked into the dining room. A little less tense now that their plan was in motion, Bennett was still anxious that someone would question why tonight there were two extra waiters. He could not believe his luck when a man, clearly in charge of the waiters, said to him, "Thank goodness you are here, we were short staffed the last three nights."

Relief rushed through his body from his ears all the way to his toes, but he tried not to let it show. His eyes took in the rows upon rows of tables neatly set with utensils and napkins. "The tables look so nice and inviting," he said.

"Ye've noticed 'ow we got the napkins out proper. Makes it all more civilized." The headwaiter beamed.

Suddenly a bell rang, the door opened, and people of all shapes and sizes, dressed in all kinds of clothing, flooded in. The calm and order was shattered in an instant. There were people everywhere, rushing for seats. Bennett looked at Tom and they sprang into action. Tom manned the milk and water jugs and Bennett started dishing out stew and potatoes. Alicia rushed from one to the other, floating plates for Bennett, so they were easier for him to balance in one hand to load the good-smelling, steaming stew with the other, and then zipped toward Tom, unobtrusively sliding glasses closer on the table, to make it easier for him to fill them with water.

All at once Tom stood stock-still. Bennett got hopeful. Maybe he saw his mother!

Tom closed his eyes. "That's strange," thought Bennett. He paused in mid-ladle, gravy dripping all over the tablecloth, staring at Tom across the room.

Tom sniffed the air. "Ahhh, a wee bit o'heaven!" and he drew in a deep satisfied breath.

What the heck is he doing? Bennett thought. Suddenly Tom rushed over to another waiter, shoved the jug of milk and the jug of water in the bewildered waiter's hands and made a beeline right toward Bennett.

"Whaaaat is going on?" Bennett asked. But then he looked at the huge bowl of mashed potatoes right at his own elbow. Tom hustled right over to it. Bennett grinned and handed him another ladle.

With an answering grin Tom said, "I'm dishing the lumpers. 'Tis the surest way to see my family; they won't be passing these tasty treats by."

Tom dished a little portion into a plate for himself. "Ah 'tis surely heaven," he said.

"What is the meaning o' this now?" said a gruff voice. The burly headwaiter had Tom by the collar.

"I was only tasting a wee pinch to make sure it was satisfactory for the diners!" protested Tom.

"I'll have to put you on report. Ye know ye don't be eating in the dining room!" exclaimed the man. "Yer'll have to wait like the rest of us to have your fill back in the kitchen. Ye know the rules." He threw down Tom's collar. Tom straightened out his jacket, lifting his head to reveal a huge toothy smile.

"How much does it take to fill up a waiter, any how?" the man muttered to himself. He ladled out a big new heaping bowl of potatoes, emptying the serving pot, and put it next to Tom with a wink. "Ye'll soon be my size if'n ye keep this up!" He hustled back into the kitchen with the empty pot.

"I've got a date with a bowl o'lumpers when serving time is over!" grinned Tom. "Eat my fill! Well, that sounds like a challenge to the likes o'me."

"Tom, FOCUS!" commanded Bennett, as the stream of diners flooded past their stations and the noise of the chatter of the many languages grew deafening.

The boys got busy serving as Tom snuck a few bites of potatoes now and then and peered anxiously at every face that appeared before him.

But the whole crowd came and went and Tom did not recognize a single face.

"Where do ye think they could be?" he asked Bennett with a sad sigh, "'tis getting pretty tiresome, getting me hopes raised, only to have them dashed all to the ground."

"They have to be here somewhere," said Bennett. "I know for certain they arrived with your sister Kate."

Tom grabbed Bennett by the starched lapels of his waiters uniform.

"Now how do you know for certain? How could you know about Kate? What have ye seen of me mother? I've a good mind to… "

Mercifully, Bennett never found out what Tom had a good mind to do, because the headwaiter shouted, "Set 'er up for the next sitting lads, and step on it. Ye know we've only fifteen minutes until they are arriving." The big man glared at the two youths.

Bennett whispered, "We will see them in fifteen minutes, I'm certain. Hang in there Tom."

"Hang in where?" asked Tom.

"Never mind," said Bennett, realizing that the expression would not make sense to anyone living in America in 1914, let alone a boy who learned to speak English in Ireland.

The boys hustled around, clearing the dirty dishes and utensils, stripping off the soiled white tablecloths, running to the pantry for crisply starched new ones and then flying them out over the tables. They ran back and forth to the bins of newly washed silverware, resetting the tables and crowning each place with an extraordinarily white napkin. Soon the dining room was restored to its splendor. The crew was just finishing the last table when the bell rang again and the doors opened. Again people flooded in and filled every place. Tom ran back to the big cauldron of mashed potatoes, refilled by the chefs (*magically*, Bennett thought) and began ladling portions of delicious looking mashed potatoes again.

As the hungry crowd subsided, he turned to Bennett with the saddest look Bennett had ever seen. "I dinna find me mother. I'm at me wits end with worry."

"Don't lose hope Tom. We have one more sitting to go," encouraged Bennett.

Once again the wait staff scurried around busing the dirty dishes and setting out fresh linen and silverware. Once again they finished making everything look inviting just as the bell rang and a new hungry crowd rushed in.

Tom piled plate after plate with steaming hot mashed potatoes, but after almost each one he shook his head sadly at Bennett.

Finally, when the line of hungry people waiting to be served dwindled away, he turned to Bennett and said, "She's simply vanished without a trace o'her in this country. Got any more magic ideas leprechaun?"

"How can that be?" Bennett ran his fingers through his hair in disbelief.

"Yer asking me? I dinno," said Tom.

"Are ye sure they are not here? Ye've been gone six years; maybe your mother looks different. Check this crowd again, while these people are still eating."

"I'd recognize me own mother," said Tom, insulted.

But he grabbed a jug of water and walked up and down the aisles of tables anyway, looking for his family. Sometimes he realized he had a pitcher in his hand and absentmindedly refilled someone's glass.

As Tom approached the second to last row of tables in the dining room Bennett went up to him and said, "Are you sure no one even looks remotely familiar?" Tom shook his head sorrowfully. Bennett scanned the faces in the room one more time. He pointed. "There's an Irish mother and children. Look closely at them."

Obediently, Tom walked closer to the mother and four children, but then shook his head again. "No, that's no me mother. And we've only two kids younger than Kate."

"Well, what about those kids?" asked Bennett. "Do any TWO look familiar? They could have gotten separated from your mother somehow."

"Saints preserve us! That young lad looks a wee bit like me brother Patrick; the red hair, the freckles. He looks like the right age. Mind you, when I left six years ago, he was only one year old. He certainly goes for the potatoes like he was me own brother! Oh what am I saying? I've lost me senses. Every Irish lad has a wee bit o' freckles and some reddish hair."

"Well, what about the two little girls, do either look familiar?" Bennett asked.

"I wouldn'a know. I left two days before me sister was born! Tis a pity me father couldna been assigned to this task! He was just in Ireland not nine months ago, when he was sent over on business. He went to visit them for a fortnight. He'd know what they looked like now."

Tom stuck out his chest with pride as he said, "Me father's an important man now; worked his way up from a laborer to a certified engineer, don't you know. Alas, he's working on ships at this very moment. In fact, his ship could have passed me mother's in the sea. Back over again t'the old country he is now."

"Look, Tom, let's just ask this lady if she knows who your mother is. Maybe she was on the same ship as your mother."

Tom rolled his eyes and looked doubtful.

"Tom! If love of potatoes is a family trait, that boy and that girl," Bennett pointed, "would definitely be related to you." Bennett then pointed to the other two children sitting with the lady. "Those two kids are probably not related. Not even distantly." The other boy and girl still had a whole lump of potatoes on their plates; the girl had not even touched them, but was devouring the stew.

"What have we got to lose?" Bennett argued. He gave Tom a gentle shove in the back. "Come on! We are running out of options."

Tom cleared his throat and said, "Pardon me, madam." When the woman turned around, he hesitated. "Would ye be needin' more water to wash them fine potatoes down?"

Bennett nudged him, and Tom almost spilled the water.

"Oh, all right," Tom said. " By chance were ye on the ship CEDRIC out of Shannon?"

"Aye, that I were!" exclaimed the woman with a smile.

"Would ye happen to know Noreen McGlew, and her brood?"

"Me own sister!"

"Aunt Kathleen!"

"Why Thomas Charles McGlew, I wouldn't 'a known ye at all. Quite the young man you have become! America's been good for you, don't you know. Let me look at you." The woman jumped up and gave him a hug. Then she held him at arm's length.

"But Aunt Kathleen, where is me mother?

"The officials detained her due to her confinement," replied Aunt Kathleen, sitting herself down.

Tom scratched his head, and looked at Bennett for an explanation.

Bennett shrugged and raised his hands.

"She's in hospital," Aunt Kathleen said, as she leaned over to scold one of the children for having their elbows on the table. "We are not animals, dearie," she said to the offender, but softened her words with a crinkling smile.

Tom's face went white. "Not me mother too! Will she recover? How gravely is her future in jeopardy?"

"A bit!" laughed Aunt Kathleen. "It'll be giving your father another mouth to feed, for many years. Looks a bit grim for the pocketbook, don't you know."

Tom looked bewildered. He again looked to Bennett for clarification. Again Bennett shrugged his shoulders.

Suddenly Tom burst out in an angry laugh, "Yer a coldhearted aunt if'n you can laugh when me mother's health is compromised."

"Tommy, me boy, she is right as rain now!" Aunt Kathleen laughed outright at his red-faced anger and confusion. "She and her little companion. We've got another member o' the clan."

"But how did...? But when did...?" Tom stuttered the start of a series of questions, but never really asked anything. "Are ye sure she is alright?"

"She is a fair bit better now than she was during the whole journey," Aunt Kathleen kept smiling and laughing. "Yer mother delivered you a wee little sister this morning!"

Tom grabbed his head. Then he started laughing.

"Don't laugh so fast," said Aunt Kathleen.

Tom immediately looked grim again.

"I'm just pointing out ye still have a reason to be angry. Yer may look all fit and American but yer new sister is already a citizen!"

Tom's face contorted with confusion. He looked at Bennett.

Bennett grinned, "This one I CAN help you with. Children born on United States soil automatically become U.S. citizens, even if their parents are not citizens."

"Well it just so happens this is one inequality I am content ta live with," laughed Tom. "But what happened to me other siblings?"

Aunt Kathleen's face lost her smile, "Kate was taken to the contagious ward and we've no message as to her condition."

"Kate is fine," Bennett burst in, "recuperating nicely."

"But where is Pat? Where is Maureen?" said Tom.

"Eating their lumpers, clean to the bowl," laughed Kathleen. "As ye can plainly see for your own self."

The four children sitting at the table all stared at Bennett and Tom with big eyes.

"Patty me boy, Maureen," said Tom with a huge grin. Two of the children ducked their heads shyly but grinned back.

Suddenly Pat jumped up from his chair and on to the back of Tom. "Tom, war it really you? I don't recognize ye at all. But yer voice sounds a bit familiar."

Tom burst out laughing, and his newly found siblings joined him, until Bennett tugged at Tom's sleeve. "See here, contain yer joy. We're getting the evil eye from the headwaiter."

"Goodness. It don't make no never mind to me now. I've got me family!" said Tom and he picked up his sister in his arms.

"Not all of it now Tom," said Bennett, still tugging his arm. "And what can you do with them now? Don't forget, we are all on the INSIDE right now. We have to be real careful, so's not to arouse suspicion. We must allow everyone to finish their dinner and go back to their dormitory to get a good night sleep. Meanwhile you and I will check to see if you can claim your family in the morning."

Tom looked doubtful. He did not make a move to stop hugging his little brother and sister. Alicia started making warning clicks of her tongue.

"Tom, com'on!" said Bennett. "Whisper to them that you will try to arrange to get permission to bring them to their new home in the morning."

Reluctantly, Tom pulled Maureen's arms off his neck and slid his sister back into her seat. He shimmied his brother off his back and pulled him around for one more quick hug.

Aunt Kathleen said, "And here's your cousins Mary and Michael."

Tom and Bennett nodded hello.

"Aunt Kathleen, I am here to claim you as my kin and escort you home," Tom announced. "We only donned these disguises because I have been here for two days and could no find a clue of yer whereabouts. Now that I know yer safe, and well looked after, I'll go back home to work 'til I get the telegram to come get ye."

Alicia waived her wand and stopped time. Everyone in the dining room froze in place.

Bennett said, "Now what is it?"

"We don't want Tom to leave without his family. If he does, there will be another mishap that we will not be able to prevent! Tell them you are privy to some information that says they will all be released tomorrow."

"But how can that be?" asked Bennett.

Pop! Alicia had on an old fashioned white powdered wig, the type lawyers still wear in England in courtrooms today, and a flowing black robe. "On information and belief, with a cross reference to the date, I can inform you that both Mrs. McGlew and Kate will be released from the hospital tomorrow afternoon. It is your job to convince Tom that he should not go home to wait for them, but should wait right here." Pop! Alicia got so excited about what she was saying to Bennett, she got herself all wound up. Literally! She flew around so fast while she was talking that her stomach looked like a corkscrew.

POP. Alicia unwound.

Before Bennett could say anything, ZAAAAP! time was unfrozen and Tom finished saying goodbye to Aunt Kathleen and the four children. Tom's family, along with the rest of the remaining detainees, straggled out of the dining room. Bennett stood there with his mouth open and tried to think of something to say.

Tom turned to leave with the immigrants. Bennett opened his mouth, still unsure what to say to change Tom's mind.

Whap! A big hand with hairy knuckles reached out and clamped down on Tom's shoulder.

"Where do ye think you're going?" said a gruff voice.

Tom turned with surprise written all over his face. "What's it to you?"

"Yer job, son! As you know yer responsibilities don't end when the dinners are over. There is a little matter of the clean up. Many a dirty dish is awaiting in the kitchen with yer name on it. Now hop to it."

Tom opened his mouth, as if to argue with the man, but Bennett grabbed his arm and pulled him along to the kitchen. Bennett looked up at Alicia flying above them with a silent plea for help: it was bad enough that they had to work their tails off setting up the dinner and serving it when there was the promise of meeting Tom's family, but now that their mission was accomplished, and they were bone tired, did they really still have to do all the dishes?

"Pssst, Alicia, a little help?" said Bennett.

"What are ye saying boy?" asked the gruff man. "Yer be as delinquent as yer chum here. I didna see you running to the kitchen to get on the cleaning when the meal was finished. Get crackn' will ya?"

"Freeze time!" whispered Bennett.

Tom let out a moan that sounded like real pain as the door opening on the messy kitchen revealing many sinks overflowing with hundreds and hundreds of dirty dishes.

Mercifully, Alicia stopped time with a quick zap of her wand.

"Whoa. Alicia – look at those dishes! You gotta help us. We can't do all those! It will take us two weeks," Bennett moaned.

"Believe it or not, they DO have a machine that helps them." At Bennett's skeptical look Alicia said, "After all, this is 1914. The steam engine has already been invented. But do not fear! The boys that are SUPPOSED to be here are lounging in the pantry, unsure why no one has started looking for them yet. Take Tom into the pantry, while I shoo the other boys out to do the dishes and we will move on with our mission."

With a big grin of relief, and a wink for Tom, Bennett shepherded him into the pantry as soon as Alicia unfroze time.

"Where ye be going?" growled the big man.

"To get more soap and rubber gloves, of course," said Bennett.

"Nice touch," whispered Alicia, "I'd better make sure your replacement crew finds the soap and wears gloves."

Alicia twinkled around the stacks of supplies and found two boys smoking cigarettes in the back of the pantry. She tried to will the boys to get back to work. They did not move toward the kitchen. Neither boy paid any attention to the angry spark flying close to their faces. Alicia screeched to a halt. Bennett looked on with amazement as Alicia's normally blue hair and wings changed inch by inch to a fiery red. He was just about to offer to tell the boys to get back to work himself when Alicia began to execute a series of cartwheels that turned into sparkly skywriting.

One boy punched the other, "I'll be a monkey's uncle! Will you give a gander at that?"

The sparkly air writing said: PICK UP THE SOAP AND GET INTO THE KITCHEN! NOW! IF YOU DON'T WANT TO BE FIRED and DEPORTED!

The other boy rubbed his eyes. "Don't know why no one has cottoned on to us yet, but I'm not heeding some sparkling sign in the air."

Pop! Alicia blew a firecracker off the top of her head. The two lazy boys jumped up. Tom's mouth dropped open. Bennett laughed.

Pop POP POP CRACKLE FIZZ FIZZ FIZZ. Alicia sent a steady stream of fireworks into the air. Limbs flailing in all directions, fear in their eyes, the delinquent boys looked at each other, rubbed their eyes and then looked back at the skywriting.

DON'T FORGET THE RUBBER GLOVES. Alicia resumed her skywriting, putting pinwheels shooting sparkles at the end of the words.

"Let's go," the lazy boys shouted. They grabbed the soap canister and rubber gloves on their way out of the pantry and ran into the kitchen.

Bennett kept laughing. "Almost as good as the 4th of July," he said, slapping Tom on the back.

"Where did those come from?" said Tom. "That display was even grander than the Croton-on-Hudson celebration."

"Yes, and the fireworks freed us from having to do the dishes," said Bennett. "Come along, we have one more stop on our mission."

CHAPTER TWELVE

One Last Twist

Enjella touched Abigail on the elbow. Suddenly it was dark.

"Now WHEN are we?" asked Abigail.

"About four hours after Bennett and Alicia left Ward Eight. The children's dinner has been removed and the ward is closed down for the night. The children are supposed to be sleeping," said Enjella.

"Do they have to lower that gate? Now it looks like the girls are in prison," said Abigail with a worried frown.

Suddenly, outside the gate, a little boy ran by. He laughed as he sped down the corridor.

Both girls turned their heads and looked. Abigail appeared in between their beds.

"That happens every night!" exclaimed Hilda.

"He's having a bit o' fun," said Kate.

"Let's go see where he is going!" said Abigail. The girls exchanged reluctant glances, but Kate stuck her foot out of the blankets, and began to climb out of the bed.

"Nein," said Hilda. "Das ist verboten!" which Abigail heard as "No! That is forbidden!"

"I don't think any harm can come from trying to see where he is going. We just want to make sure he is alright," Abigail smiled and Kate grinned back impishly.

Hand in hand, Abigail and Kate walked to the gate with quiet, careful steps.

CLACKETY CLACK!

"UUUH," both girls jumped at the racket. Kate had rattled the gate a little as she tried to see if she could lift the slats open.

The girls looked around nervously, but the corridor in front of them and the ward behind them remained silent. Hilda watched from the safety of her bed with eyes rounded and enlarged by apprehension.

With one more anxious glance behind her, Abigail bent down and pulled at the bottom of the gate. More easily than she expected, the gate lifted!

Kate and Abigail looked at each other with astonishment.

"If I'da known 't would be done so surely, I woulda tried much before today," whispered Kate.

Silently, the gate slid upward with ease. Abigail held it up just enough for the two girls and the Fairy to slip underneath.

Abigail's heart was still pounding, but she smiled and whispered, "That was easy," as the gate dropped noiselessly back to the floor.

"Sure! But me heart is still stuck in me mouth, as if I had seen Saint Brigid's ghost herself," Kate whispered back.

The girls looked left and then right down the long corridor.

"Look!" Kate pointed. At the end of the corridor was the boy. He was looking out the window. They turned and ran to see what he was looking at. There was the Statue of Liberty, her torch lit and glowing in the starry night. The girls leaned against the window and drew in their breath with delight. Their wonder and awe at this beautiful sight made their eyes glow like Lady Liberty's torch.

"She is welcoming us," said Kate. Abigail smiled and squeezed her hand.

"OOOO, stars," said Abigail. "It is amazing how many more stars I can see, right over the New York Harbor. I wonder why I can't usually see this many stars from my bedroom?"

"Light pollution," said Bennett in her ear. Abigail jumped in surprise and turned her head quickly to see Bennett smiling at her. "We have too many lights on at night in the 21st Century. Didn't you ever notice the orange glow over New York City?"

"Where did you come from?" said the startled Abigail.

"Tommy and I took the ferry that Ellis Island runs between the main administrative building and the hospital so people can visit their relatives.

"At night?" asked Alicia.

"We caught the last one, ferrying employees and immigrants back from hospital visiting hour. Of course we had to sneak around a bit to get into the contagious ward, but, no harm no foul! We are getting good at sneaking around, since we managed to visit Tom's relatives in the dining room," said Bennett.

"Who's Tom?" Abigail asked.

Bennett and Tom stepped up to the window and leaned on their elbows next to the Italian boy who had run past. They pointed at the Statue.

"The Grand Lady!" said the boy. "Right here in front of our window. Promising us liberty."

"Bennett! Who is that?" asked Abigail, pointing to Tom.

"See who I found?" said Bennett, with a wink. But just as Bennett had not recognized Tommy at first, neither did Abigail. Kate certainly did not either. She looked over at Tom with a mild curiosity, but nothing more. She looked back at the Statue of Liberty and sighed dreamily.

Tom started whistling, "When Irish Eyes are Smiling."

A light bulb went off in Abigail's head. She and Bennett began singing along. "Sure 'tis like a morning spring..."

Tom broke off his whistling and looked at Abigail in surprise and then laughed. "What have we here, another leprechaun? Is America full of magical creatures?" Tom looked over at Kate, who was not singing. "Are ye not a leprechaun too?"

Abigail and Bennett exchanged a surprised look.

With a twinkle in his eye Bennett said with a bow, "Thomas Charles McGlew, may I present your sister, Kathryn Alice McGlew!"

Brother and sister gasped, just alike. They both colored red from their freckled chins to the roots of their red hair. Coloring and mannerisms were so alike; there was no denying that they were related. Then they both laughed.

Laughing, hugging and kissing, Tom said, "I thought you looked familiar. You look like me. You even laugh like me!"

Bennett and Abigail hooted and slapped each other's hands. Enjella and Alicia gave each other the WINGS UP sign.

"How are ye here? Where did ye come from? Where is Pa? How are ye so fit?" Kate fired one question after another.

"Fit as a fiddle," smiled her brother. "I found ye at last, thanks to this wee leprechaun. There was gold at the end of his mischievous rainbow – the treasure of being reunited with me family."

"Alas, 'tis only me," said Kate, her sadness returning. "I've no seen mother since the Grand Hall where I was chalk-marked and identified with the sickness. I do not know the fate of mother, Patrick and wee Maureen."

"Thanks to me leprechaun, I do," laughed Tom. "First he helped me find Aunt Kathleen and our kin. They were feasting on lumpers in the dining room, don't you know. Next, this magical fella got us on a ferry to Mother's hospital ward..."

"Hospital?" screeched Kate, as the blood drained from her face.

Bennett opened his mouth, bursting to tell Kate of their adventures and the new addition to the family, but Enjella gave him a warning look. "It is not our story to tell," Enjella whispered.

"Now don't be jumping to conclusions before ye hear me through," laughed Tom and gave her a hug. "'Tis wonderful news. You've a new sister to love and a mother right as rain and ready to start her new life in America."

"When? Where? How did Aunt Kathleen..." stammered Kate.

"I've learned a thing or two about the generous people in our new country. There are quite a number of humanitarians that can aide us with your medical expenses. Mother has been given the finest of care, as have you."

"Ah!" a small voice sounded at Kate's elbow. Everyone turned around.

"Hilda!" said Kate.

"You have joined us," said Abigail to Hilda in German.

"The statute! Her torch is lighted. She looks so welcoming," said Hilda in German. "I am so glad to see…"

"Me hope is restored," declared Kate. "Lady Liberty is shining a welcome light on our path. Soon we will be looking at her from the other side of the river, when we start our new life in New York."

"Ja, I very much want quickly to see New York," said Hilda in English. "I someday hope that beautiful new building to see." Hilda pointed to the New York City skyline, faintly visible behind The Statute of Liberty, where a tall building shone like a beacon, bright with electric light.

"Wunderbar," said Abigail. "Your English is already so good."

"That architectural beauty is the new Woolworth building," announced Tom, as proud as if he had built it himself. "It was just completed this month."

"Sehr hubsch! Magical," sighed Hilda. "Every day English I will practice. With quickness I will American sound," she said with a smile.

"Here's an American sound!" grinned Tom, "Not as new as 'Irish Eyes'– This song's music was written in 1883 and the poem was written in 1904. But the words and lyrics together as a song called 'America the Beautiful' was just published in 1910. I wonder if ye know it?"

Bennett and Abigail nodded.

"A course ye do," smiled Tom. They all burst into song: "O beautiful for spacious skies, for amber waves of grain," sang Tom. Bennett and Abigail smiled at each other as they sang along. Hilda and Kate started to hum the melody. Kate reached out and grabbed Hilda's hand and gave it a squeeze.

Bennett and Abigail looked around at the group and at the Statue of Liberty. Every word of the song took on new significance. Tom knew all four verses. Bennett and Abigail kept singing along even though Bennett was pretty sure he had never even heard verse three.

"He sings as much as Grandpa!" Bennett whispered to Abigail in between stanzas.

They were three quarters of the way through the song again; "Till all success be nobleness…" when Abigail leaned back and saw Hilda and Kate were still holding hands, with tears in their eyes, looking at the shining torch of the Statue.

ZAAAAAP! The light from the torch of the Statue of Liberty faded and Bennett and Abigail were whisked away again.

Bennett and Abigail blinked hard in the bright light of their bedroom.

Abigail sighed. They were back in the 21st century, far away in time and space from Ellis Island and their new friends.

"AWWWW. I HATE it when you do that!" said Bennett. "I want to get to know them better. I want to see them reunite with their families. I want to make sure they all get off Ellis Island alright. How can you pull us away from our adventure at a time like this?"

"We are missing the best part," agreed Abigail.

"Not true!" said Enjella and Alicia together.

"We have experienced the best part right along with the immigrants we came to help," said Enjella.

"We let you stay through ALL the stanzas of *America the Beautiful*," reasoned Alicia.

"Yes, you were on the third verse for the second time," confirmed Enjella.

"But Tom, Kate and Hilda will notice we are gone," said Bennett.

"They will think it strange that we just disappeared," said Abigail with a vigorous shake of her head.

"I can hear it now. When they discover you are gone, Hilda and Kate will say that you were called to help someone else and Tom will say…" said Enjella.

"I knew the wee fella was a leprechaun!" finished Enjella and Alicia together.

Bennett and Abigail realized this was true.

"You can picture the rest of their stories in your imagination. The next day both Hilda and Kate are well enough to leave. They are reunited with their families right at the Kissing Post." Enjella hugged herself at the thought. Alicia fluttered a WINGS UP sign.

"But what happens then?" asked Abigail.

"Yeah," said Bennett, "where do they go? What becomes of them?"

"Your great grandmother Hilda settles in New York City with her family, and eventually becomes president of the ladies board of the Leo House, the aide society that helped post her bond."

"I knew Hilda sounded familiar. I don't think I got to meet her — before tonight that is. I guess I was too young. But she looked a little like my grandmother," said Bennett.

"Yes, and the songs she sang in the hospital were the same ones Grammy sings to us when she visits," said Abigail.

"What about Kate, what happened to her?"

"She is your great great grandfather's sister. It is Tom that you are directly related to," said Enjella. "He is your great great grandfather."

"What a friendly man. Now I know why Grandpa is always singing, and is such an optimist," smiled Abigail.

"Are you sure we can't go back to 1914?" asked Bennett. "It sure was fun making life easier for great great grandfather Tom," said Bennett.

"Yes," agreed Abigail. "It was quite the adventure to be able to meet and help some of our ancestors."

"We saw so many people who had such hard lives. I was glad you were able to help at least some of them get through such a difficult experience more easily," said Enjella.

Bennett said, "Our great grandmother Sarah was so brave! Leaving her homeland all by herself and traveling to a strange place she had never seen without speaking a word of English! That's a lot of chutzpah!"

Alicia did a cartwheel, "I see the adventure at Ellis Island is continuing to improve your vocabulary!" Pop! A dictionary appeared on her head with "chutzpah, Yiddish *nerve, gall, audacity*" highlighted and in bold type.

Bennett laughed. "More importantly, I now know none of us would be who we are today without the courage and sacrifices that our immigrant ancestors made."

"Yes," agreed Abigail, "while we did not have to make their sacrifices, nor be as brave, I think our small part of giving them kindness helped. It was amazing to see all the good that was done there by others too — the volunteers from the Aide societies and the hard working staff at Ellis Island."

"Your great grandmother Hilda never forgot it. After she settled in

America and began to prosper, she spent many years of her life working with and supporting The Leo House and all their efforts to help new immigrants," reminded Enjella.

"Did she ever get to go into the Woolworth building?" asked Abigail.

Enjella shook her head 'yes' and said, 'Nein'!

"Only kidding! Yes. In fact, not only did she see it when she was young, but later in life her husband, your great grandfather, established his law office there."

"Do you think Kate and Hilda ever saw each other again?" asked Bennett.

"Yes they did," said Alicia.

"I just remembered!" exclaimed Abigail. "Grandpa told us that his father met his mother at the German Turnverein Society social!"

Bennett scratched his head. "That doesn't make sense! Our great grandparents on Grandpa McGlew's side were both Irish. What were they doing at a German society?"

Abigail laughed, "That's just what I asked Grandpa. His answer: his Irish parents lived in a German neighborhood, and the Turnverein was where everyone hung out. Great grandpa McGlew even knew a few phrases in German."

"I guess America has always been called a 'melting pot' of people and cultures," smiled Enjella. Pop! A big bubbling cauldron appeared over her head. Alicia flew up to it, turned her wand into a stick and started stirring it.

"We just got to see our ancestors, the ingredients, before they melted," said Bennett with a sparkling spin.

"No!" said Abigail, "with a little kindness, we got to help some of them melt!"

The Fairies spun the children around in a floating group hug encircled with sparkles. They landed in their own beds, and sighed a sigh of happiness and accomplishment.

As they said, "Good night," to their Fairies, the eyes of the children closed and the Fairies tapped them with a magic spell to lull them to sleep.

The Fairies flashed each other the WINGS UP sign.

With a flourish of sparkles the two Elbow Fairies disappeared and the two children smiled in their sleep.

Glossary of Magic Words

Immigrant. someone who comes INTO a country to settle there

Emigrant. someone who LEAVES a country to go live in another country

WINGS UP. the sign the Fairies make when they greet or congratulate each other. *(To make the WINGS UP sign: hold both your hands in front of you, palms facing toward you. Cross your hands over each other and link your thumbs. Then waive your fingers.)*

CHAPTER ONE

Conscientious. careful, thorough, diligent

Unperturbed. calm, unworried

Scrutinized. examined closely

Apparel. clothing

Dirndl dress. a dress with a full gathered skirt, the traditional dress of Germany & Austria

Pirouetting. spinning, usually on the tip of the toe

Elementary. basic, uncomplicated, straight forward

Shenanigans. mischief

Flurry. a short period of time when a lot of things happen

Lamented. mourned, grieved, bemoaned

CHAPTER TWO

Imposing. impressive, intimidating, scary

Foreboding. apprehension

Piling. support, column or structure, usually made of wood, which holds up a pier

Gangplank. small portable bridge

Simultaneously. at the same time

Debris. garbage

Peninsulas. narrow pieces of land that jut out from the mainland into a sea or lake

Chortled. laughed in a noisy gleeful way

Gloated. expressed smug self-satisfaction, lorded it over them!

Inquisitive. curious, interested, inquiring

Cohort. a supporter, helper or accomplice

CHAPTER THREE

Chalk Markings:
B = back
C = eye condition
Ct = trachoma
Ex = examine further
Ft = feet
H = heart
K = hernia
L = lameness
Pg = pregnant
S = senility
X = feeble mind or insanity

Stairs of Separation. the name given to the flight of stairs at the end of the Registry room that lead to different destinations

Resounded. ring out loudly, resonate, boom, reverberate

Emanated. came out of something

Contraption. machine, especially one that seems strange

Oblivion. the state of being utterly forgotten

Laboriously. with great difficulty

Chaotic. confused, hectic

Intelligible. understandable, comprehensible

Clerical. relating to office work or routine administrative work

Manifest. the written record of the ship listing all of the passengers and their answers to the immigration questions

Assimilate. minimize the differences between themselves and their new countrymen, integrate

Ikh shoyn fargesin. Yiddish word for 'I already forgot'

Indignantly. in annoyance, crossly

Mischievously. playfully, with a twist of naughtiness

Foreshadow. predict, foretell

Invalids. sick people

Rickets. a disease caused by a vitamin D deficiency, affecting mostly children, that makes bones soft, and changes skeletal structure

Lame. unable to walk, having diseases of the legs

Garbled. jumbled, confused

Niceties. a feature that makes something pleasurable or pleasant

Deduction. a conclusion drawn from available information

Detainment. the state of being held in custody

Nuisance. annoyance, irritation

CHAPTER FOUR

Trifle. small, hardly worth noticing

Bewildered. extremely confused

Cogitate. think, ponder

Apt. appropriate

Metaphor. image, comparison

Detained. held back, prevented from leaving

Mein Nommen ist. German/Yiddish for 'my name is'

Linguistics. the study of language

Absentmindedly. without thinking

Leafing. riffling through

Betrothed. fiancé, the person to whom someone is engaged to be married

Elocution. diction, pronunciation

Carfare. money for transportation

Corroborating. confirming

Notarized. verified, certified that it is accurate

Entrepreneurship. free enterprise, working hard

Chutzpah. Yiddish word adopted into American English meaning 'spunk, nerve, gall'

Merriment. high spirits, happiness

Ikh bin. Yiddish words for 'I am'

CHAPTER FIVE

Plied. used a tool in a skillful way

Buttonhook. a device that looked like a rod with a hook at the end of it intended for pulling the buttons on tight boots into place for fastening

Barbaric. uncivilized, unsophisticated

Trachoma. a contagious bacterial eye disease in which scar tissue forms inside the eyelid, causing it to curve inward and the eyelashes to scrape the eye, sometimes causing blindness or death

Inflammation. swelling, irritation

Liability. problem, burden, responsibility

O Sole Mio. Italian Song 'O My Soul'

Certamente. Italian for 'certainly'

Securemente. Italian for 'surely'

Pronto. Italian for 'right away'

Bambino. Italian for 'baby'

Sporadically. periodically, occasionally

Puckered. wrinkled, creased, furrowed

CHAPTER SIX

Arduous. requiring hard work or continuous strenuous effort

Corroborate. verify

Culminating. reaching the highest point, ending

Copious. abundant, plentiful

Blared. made a loud harsh noise

Veracity. truth

Impaired. Weakened, worsened

Locomotion. movement from one place to another

Endeavored. tried

Matron. a woman on the staff to supervise and help unattended children and women

Transporting. carrying people or goods from one place to another

Reassured. comforted

Perplexed. confused

Facilitate. make easier

Speculated. guessed

Jilted. abruptly broke a promise to marry someone

Destitute. very poor, penniless

CHAPTER SEVEN

Gizmo. a gadget

Ingenious. clever, original

Observant. paying such careful attention that nothing goes unnoticed

Contagious. infectious, catching

CHAPTER EIGHT

Rakish. jaunty, casual, stylish

Lagoon. a coastal body of shallow water

Allocate. to set aside for a particular purpose

Precarious. unstable, shaky

Fritter. waste, squander, dribble away, dissipate,

Collateral. security, guarantee

Delicatessen. now just called 'deli', a store specializing in imported cooked meats, cheeses, and pickles

Urchin. rascal, brat

Fatality. death

Autoclave. large steel machine that sterilizes

Mutely. without a sound, wordlessly

Petrified. scared stiff!, frightened

Fretted. worried

CHAPTER NINE

Hubbub. noise, racket, din

Summons. call, order, command

Clamored. demanded noisily, shouted

Arduous. hard, difficult

CHAPTER TEN

Digress. to wander from the subject and start talking about something else

Frivolous. unnecessary

Melodramatic. exaggerated, theatrical

Candy striper. a young volunteer worker in a hospital

Ja. German word for 'yes'

Nein. German word for 'no'

CHAPTER ELEVEN

Contorted. twisted, distorted.

Intoned. to say something in a slow, serious way

Burly. heavily built, robust, broad shouldered

Indubitably. undoubtedly, definitely

Saddled. burdened with a task or responsibility

Distress. concern, worry, grief, misery

Contrite. sorry, apologetic

Rectify. correct, remedy, cure

Victuals. food

Uncharacteristically. unusually, abnormally

Don. to put on

Unobtrusively. inconspicuously, shyly

Magnificence. grandeur, luxury

Subsided. became less active, sunk, dropped

Absentmindedly. inattentively, without thinking

Fortnight. a United Kingdom expression meaning a period of 14 days

Devouring. eating something quickly and hungrily

Hesitated. paused, uncertain

Brood. children, family

Confinement. old fashioned way to say a women going into labor

Gravely. seriously

Bewildered. confused, puzzled

Clarification. explanation

Compromise. finding a middle ground

Arouse. awaken, alert

Reluctantly. unwillingly, halfheartedly

Shimmied. moved in a shaking or swaying way, climbed

Mishap. an unfortunate accident or piece of luck

Privy. knowing something secret or private

Detainees. people held in custody, not free to leave

Straggled. strayed from the path, coming or going in a disorganized way

Delinquent. neglecting a duty or responsibility

Gander. a look or glance at something

Cottoned. caught on

Heeding. paying serious attention to

Squinted. looked through narrowed eyes

Apprehension. anxiety, fear

CHAPTER TWELVE

Reluctant. hesitant, unwilling

Das ist Verboten. German for 'that is forbidden'

Impishly. devilishly

Shepherded. herded, guided

Mannerisms. gestures, traits, characteristics

Stanzas. verses of a song

Turnverein Society. German American organization which supported immigrants and provided cultural and social gatherings

Cauldron. a large metal pot in which liquids are boiled

Author's Note

This Enjella tale is based on a compilation of the many many great stories of the people who immigrated to the United States in the last two centuries.

I have taken great poetic license with the stories of the people named in this adventure. Sometimes I have used complete stories, sometimes I have only used people's names attached to a compilation of stories and sometimes I have made up characters completely. And of course I have twisted time! The McGlews and the Schweigers did not immigrate in the same year.

Some stories I found intact, preserved from start to finish in one book or another. Other stories only revealed themselves in bits and pieces. By interviewing friends and relatives and searching out immigrant stories both oral and written, I have gleaned many more pieces of the puzzle.

This Enjella Adventure seeks to emphasize the positive aspects of the processing of immigrants through Ellis Island. Yes, certainly, many tears were shed here, but there were far many more happy stories. The final statistics show that only 2% of the hundreds of thousands of immigrants who came to America during the entire time Ellis Island was opened were turned away. The state of the art hospitals and the dedicated doctors and nurses saved many lives. The many volunteers helped many a poor and frightened immigrant navigate the often-confusing process and settle into their new life. Most of the people who worked for or were connected to Ellis Island did their best job. Some of the names of the outstanding people are mentioned here. But there were also many unsung heroes who changed immigrants' lives for the better.

Some of the real names used in this story, and the fragments of their real story that I know are as follows:

Hilda Schweiger, her sister Cilly and her mother Caecillia – the manifest from their ship the SS Chemnitz confirms that they all arrived on June 25, 1914. Hilda celebrated her 12th birthday on board the ship, even though the manifest says she was 12 years and 6months old. Her mother, Caecillia has her name spelled "Cacillia" which is not how my mother (Hilda's daughter) said it was spelt. Also, "Cilly" must have had a real name. I knew her as "Auntie". They traveled second class. I do not know if they came through Ellis Island. Hilda (my grandmother) did have the measles at some point in her life. She was hospitalized as in the story but her hospitalization could have been in Vienna, Austria. The girl in the bed next to her there could have been the one who shook her head "no" for "Ja" or "yes" and "yes" for "Nein" or " no". Hilda did grow up to be on the board and also the president of the Leo House on 23rd St in New York City. Whether or not the Leo House helped with her immigration I do not know.

Sarah Dirdack was my husband's Grandmother. She was betrothed to B.W. or Bill Cohen. (His real name is uncertain. Family history says it was Velvul Kagan who became Cohen when he immigrated.) My husband's Grandfather Bill sent the money for Sarah's passage and the instructions "Come to Massachusetts." Sarah made the trip from her homeland, perhaps in Belarus, all the way to Holyoke Massachusetts, all by herself without speaking a word of English. I could not find any record of Sara Dirdack in the Ellis Island manifest records, but I did find several variations of the spelling in different years arriving from "Baregin" and other countries in that area, whose nationality was simply listed as "Hebrew" departing from Antwerp.

B.W. Cohen – It is difficult to ascertain exactly what my husband's grandfather's last name was. I will keep searching! The family story: B.W. or Bill came through Ellis Island, had his name changed from Velvul Kagan to Benjamin William Cohen. He started earning a living right away as a peddler, with his wares on his back. He was hard working and enterprising. As his number of children grew he graduated to owning a cart to carry his wares and a horse named Napoleon. Bill would spur the horse into quickening its pace by saying, "Giddy-up Napolean, it looks like rain." Bill's acumen and accomplishments grew until he finally owned and operated a successful men's clothing store.

McGlew – The McGlews probably came to America in the late 1800s after the potato famines in Ireland. The records of the McGlew immigration were probably lost in the fire that burned the first building at Ellis Island to the ground, destroying everything in it. However, I did find a Charles McGlew, nationality Irish, arrived from Liverpool on Dec 6, 1914 on the SS SAINT PAUL.

Sam Koren was the boy who thought America had a lot of legs. Uncle Sam was one of the many who tasted white bread for the first time in his life at Ellis Island.

Madeline Zeidan – arrived in 1956, one of the last years that Ellis Island was opened. She recalled how foreboding the main building looked, dark and gloomy. She was a beautiful blonde haired twelve-year-old and her mother was dark haired. They questioned both women as to whether Madeline was really her mother's daughter. She recalls the whole processing only taking a few hours. When they were seated in the dining room having dinner, her father arrived to pick them up and take them to their new home.

Illustrator Bio

London native, David Trumble is an international award-winning cartoonist, author and illustrator, who rose to critical acclaim at the age of 21 as the youngest political cartoonist to work at London's Sun Newspaper. Trumble currently works as both an illustrator and author, having sold nearly a million children's books. In addition, he writes and draws satirical cartoons for the Huffington Post, which have garnered millions of views, and been featured internationally through media outlets that include The Today Show, Upworthy, NBS's iVillage, The Christian Science Monitor, Jezebel, The Boston Globe and The Sunday Times in the UK. Described as a "mega-watt talent" and a "consummate professional" by publishers, Trumble's illustrations for a Simon & Schuster book soared to the number one spot on Amazon's "Mover & Shaker" list. David has been the keynote speaker on two TED talks and has lectured to children in both US and UK schools on the subject of creativity.

Author Bio

Jane F. Collen is a lawyer specializing in Intellectual Property Law. Her avocation to write children's books began at night. The award winning Enjella® Adventure Series evolved from bedtime fairy tales she spun for her children. In addition to the Enjella® Adventure Series Jane has written an historical romance. She holds a BA in English and Speech Communications as well as a Juris Doctorate.

Jane lectures on Intellectual Property matters and speaks and writes about writing and children's literacy.

Jane spent a many happy hours reading all kinds of children's books to her four children. Now she volunteers at libraries and schools to read to children and spur their passion for books. Her main motive for writing the children's series was to foster the tradition of capturing children's imaginations and expanding their vocabularies through reading.

A history buff and a believer in magic, Jane loves to make up stories based on actual events in people's lives. David and Jane toured Ellis Island National Park together in preparation for writing this book.

You can find Jane and Enjella online at www.enjella.com.

www.ingramcontent.com/pod-product-compliance
Lightning Source LLC
Chambersburg PA
CBHW051838170626
46807CB00003B/1241

* 9 780985 573263 *